STANDING IN THE
SHADOWS OF FERNWOOD

BRAXTON HARRIS

authorHOUSE®

AuthorHouse™
1663 Liberty Drive
Bloomington, IN 47403
www.authorhouse.com
Phone: 1 (800) 839-8640

Published by AuthorHouse   06/29/2015

ISBN: 978-1-5049-1921-0 (sc)
ISBN: 978-1-5049-1920-3 (e)

Library of Congress Control Number: 2015910090

Print information available on the last page.

For Elks Point Lodge,

- One day you wake up and realize that life isn't about the destination, it's about the memories, and once you have those, you won't miss a thing.

#EIGHTEEN

1

On the Tenth Street and Eighth Avenue of Fernwood, there was an Eighteenth house. The house belonged to a lady named Margaret Johnson.

It was built on the grounds of a recently abandoned town, by her father in 1896, the same year she was born. There was a house that stood there before, but it was torn down a while back.

After the disaster had settled, people began to move in and repopulate the area. Bad things had happened there, nobody forgot that, they all just thought that they could try again. They ridded the land of its old name vowing to never speak of it again. Thus Fernwood was born.

Margaret's family started off large. There was Margaret, she was the youngest of them all, next up was her brother Alex who was just a year older. Two years older than him was her next brother Daniel, a year after him was her third brother Clayton. Her sister Melody was the oldest. Then of course there was here Mother Sylvia and her father. They were happy for a while, but it was just a short while, it didn't take long before everything began to fade away.

In 1905 there was a fire at the house. It started in the parent's bedroom and grew to be no more than small. They managed to extinguish it before it got out of control. It did do some serious damage to that half of the house, there was a hole burnt right through the ceiling. Alex was the only one in there when it happened. He was also the only one who didn't make it out.

Margaret was terribly upset. She wasn't familiar with death yet. When it came time for the funeral she didn't know what to do. She was sad and wanted to be alone, but there were so many people. She wasn't even sure who some of them were. There was one man there who kept staring at her the whole time. He smiled, revealing teeth of gold. It was a nice smile, but there was evil in it. She got frightened from this. She turned around and she ran, she didn't run very far, just far enough. There was a giant tree she found and thought it would be a nice place to sit under, she could hide in its shadows. When it came time for service it was Clayton who went and got her. He knew she was upset, everyone was upset. She just seemed hurt the most.

"What are you doing out here?" he asked.

"I don't want to go to the funeral, I don't like it. I just want my brother back, why can't I have my brother back?" Margaret began to cry. Clayton knelt down and offered a hug. She jumped into his arms.

"Life is complicated, it gets that way," Clayton began," there's lots of really big questions, but no answers. At times like these it's best to accept the situation. It's much easier to deal with that way."

"But there are all those people there, I don't want to see them, I don't want to talk to them. I miss my brother."

"I'll tell you what, you come there with me. I'll guide you through it. You can hold my hand. Anytime you feel scared just close your eyes. You can close your eyes and think of Alex. The good memories, you got to hold on to those. Nobody will bother you, I'll see to it, I'll just talk for you, and you can close your eyes. Your part of the family Margaret, we need you there, for Alex."

Margaret was still uncomfortable with the situation, but she was comfortable with Clayton. He would guide her through her first difficult time in life. Margaret found a new kind of respect for her brother that day. He seemed a bit more trust worthy. She was glad to have someone like him during a time like this.

They walked back to where everyone was gathered to begin the ceremony. Margaret held onto Clayton's hand the whole time. She closed her eyes when she got scared and he made it safe. He spoke for her when people wanted to talk to her, as he said he would, and then it was over. They lowered her brother into the ground and everybody walked away. She didn't think she would have made it through that day, but she did. All thanks to the guidance of her brother.

The next day, Clayton was helping their father cover the hole in the ceiling. Margaret was in the same room. She was sitting on the bed talking to her brother while he was patching the ceiling. Her father was up on the roof covering the other side. Something went wrong up there, there was a thump, and both of them heard it. They looked up as the thump turned into a slide, and then it stopped. There were a few grunts and groans, then silence.

"Are you all right up there Dad?" Clayton shouted.

"Yeah." They heard him shout back. Margaret was struck with relief and continued to brush her dolls hair. Then there was a crash. She looked up to see her father falling through the roof. There was a specific board in the roof that came loose when her father came crashing through it. The board had a nail which directed itself to a point in Clayton's eye. As it made its way there, her father came right behind it. He landed on top of his son, causing the nail to go where it was going to go a whole lot faster and with enough force to cause the most amount of damage. Two days after that Margaret had a second funeral to go to, this time without a guide.

Their mother became severely depressed. Most of her time was spent sitting in her room and crying. If they listened carefully they could hear her whispering sometimes, but there was still crying. Sometimes she would be screaming, but there was still crying. They could always hear her crying. Everybody was sad.

A week had passed. The mother continued to cry as Daniel and their father were working on the land. Melody was taking care of chores in the house while Margaret played with her dolls. The sounds of their mother were getting far too depressing. Melody didn't think it was a good idea to let Margaret be surrounded by that type of atmosphere for too long, so she decided to take Margaret for a walk. She would pack a lunch and they could go find a nice field to have a picnic. Maybe they could invite their mother out too. It might make her happy.

Melody went into her mother's room and told her about the plan. Her mother declined the offer, but told them to have a good time. Which they did.

They ran and played games, they laughed and they smiled. They had so much fun they even time slipped their mind. Margaret thought they'd be in trouble for sure going back home so late, but when they did get home, Daniel and her father were still out working in the yard. They were safe, because they were the only ones who would have noticed.

They went inside. It was quiet. It took a moment for them to realize exactly how quiet it actually was. The crying, it was done. Margaret thought that it might have been a good thing. Melody thought otherwise. Margaret was having a hard time removing her shoes, she sat down and began to struggle with the laces. Her sister plopped her shoes off without a problem and ran straight for their mother's room. Margaret eventually got her shoes off and began making her way into the same direction as her sister. As she approached the door of the bedroom her sister came walking back out with tears in her eyes. She stopped Margaret where she was and walked her back outside. She was told to wait on the porch. She did that, but not without asking a series of questions she got no answers to. So she just sat and waited.

Melody ran off into the field where her father was. Margaret couldn't hear what was being said, but it wasn't long until her father came running back towards the house. He ran up the steps, past Margaret, nearly tearing the door off its hinges on the way in. That was the third time she saw her father cry, and it was all in the same month. After that, it was just the three of them.

It stayed that way for a few years, during those years nobody was ever as happy as they could have been. Melody had been the one taking care of everybody while their father did what he could to make a dollar. Around the time when Margaret was thirteen, she noticed a change in her brother's behavior. He had a certain attitude. It came very suddenly, it was a change overnight. He became acting bad, and just like that, life had returned to terrible.

There were three times they caught him trying to kill the family dog. They would have caught him again if they hadn't all gone out. Instead they came home to find a dead dog lying in the middle of the living room. All of its guts had been ripped out and thrown everywhere. That's when they heard him laughing. They looked over to where the laughter was coming from and there he was, just sitting tucked in the corner laughing at them. He was sent away after that. She knew her sister and father had contact with him, but it was very limited. She wasn't allowed to ask any questions. If she did, everyone would start to get emotional, there'd be arguments. It would be a terrible time during terrible times. So without forgetting about him, she forgot about him.

A few years after that her sister found herself a man and moved out with him. He found himself a job in Landmark and they both moved out that way where they generated three children. Garth, Dan and Wayne. They didn't get a happily ever after, but they got close enough.

Margaret had just turned eighteen when her father had become ill. He couldn't get out of the house, then he couldn't get out of his room, then he couldn't get out of his bed. It all happened quite quickly. She was there the whole time, just her and her father in a big empty house. It wasn't long until he passed on. Her sister came back for the funeral, Margaret didn't need a guide this time, she was familiar with the procedures. Once the funeral was over, the sisters hugged and said their goodbyes. Then Margaret was left alone with the family house, and its lack of happy memories. Margaret stayed in the house, she got a job and maintained the house. Keeping to herself most of the time. She would come out and talk to the mailman if he needed to be told not to step on the grass, or if she had to speak to the parents of the children who thought it would be fun to play in her tree. That's the way she lived. She didn't like it, but at an early age she discovered life wasn't a thing you were supposed to like. It's just something that's there and needs to be dealt with.

She would see happy families all of the time. She became quite jealous of them, for having something she so much desired. This jealousy soon turned to hatred, as it quite often does. She would laugh at the family people. She would laugh because she knew the pain they would go through one day when they start to die off. These thoughts made her happy.

She talked to her sister from time to time, not as often as sisters should, but neither one of them was particularly fond of each other's lifestyle. Communication mostly consisted of letters. On average they came face to face about twice a year, for Christmas and Easter.

Time passed and she got old. Visits from her sister dwindled down to once a year. Margaret didn't like to leave the house much, so she didn't. It went on that way for five years. Then the visits from her sister stopped completely, soon after the letters stopped right along with it. It took four months before any word got around to Margaret that her sister had died. And just like that, there she was. Sixty seven years old. The last one standing.

Margaret had turned seventy six before she passed away. She sat in the house for a whole two months before anybody noticed. It was because her bills weren't getting paid. When no one could get a hold of her, police entered the building finding Margaret sitting in her rocking chair. It was rocking when they got in, one of the officers thought he saw her smile, but he blamed it on his imagination, which wasn't very imaginative.

Wayne was the youngest of her sisters children, but he was the only one who had the time. He came out there after she had passed. Her sister was initially on the will but because she was gone it went on to her children. Wayne planned on selling the house and dividing the money between the other two brothers, everybody was fine with that.

He got down there with an initial plan to stay in the house until he could take care of the things that need to be taken care of when selling a house. After the first night he decided it would be better to stay at a hotel. After the second night he wanted out of the town completely. There was a very weird vibe to it. It wasn't the people, it was something else, it was something in the air, maybe even the ground. It wasn't the right place.

He met with a man named Clark, he was a representative for the local real estate agency. They made some arrangements and then Wayne left Fernwood, without ever looking back.

Two months passed before a Chris Willshire came along with his wife Bridget and their two daughters Michelle, who was eight, and five year old Brianna. He had just got a new job in Fernwood and had planned on moving his family out there. They had a life to develop and memories to make.

They saw the eighteenth house on Tenth Street and Eighth Avenue. They thought it was a nice house. There was work that needed to be done on the house, lots of work, but they got it for a decent price. On top of that, they had their whole lives to work on it, build on to the home and their memories at the same time. Clark and the Willshire's made a deal.

When a house fails to become a vault for the finest in family memories, it fails for a reason. Reasons aren't always explained, but they're always there, and they always have their way.

2

It was the morning on the third day of summer in 1972. Two days previous, The Willshire's had just moved into their new Fernwood home.

Chris was the first one up that morning, this was usual for the Willshire family. First Chris would wake up, then Brianna, followed by Michelle and finally his wife. That was of course the way things went on the weekend. During the main part of the week it was a bit more opposite. Chris would still be the first one up, but his wife would get up with him, followed closely by the children, but this was the weekend.

He had planned on doing quite a bit today, everyone seemed to be happy with the house so far. He was up and outside working when Brianna and Michelle woke up. They started playing with their dolls. They were getting loud with them, Brianna could be heard yelling about a brush. That's when Bridget woke up. She came out into the living room to neutralize the argument that had unfolded.

"You two girls need to settle down." Bridget said.

"But she stole the brush I was using and she won't give it back," Brianna cried, "give me my brush!" "I never took your brush, you set it down behind you." Michelle reached over behind Brianna and pretended to pick up the toy brush, which was in Michelle's hand the whole time. Brianna looked at the brush, she felt uncertain about what was going on. To Bridget it looked like they would be getting along now, she turned around to return to her bedroom. Michelle took notice to her mother's lack of attention and pulled the brush away as Brianna was reaching for it. It was then thrown across the room. Michelle gave a dirty smile as Brianna made the face that a little girl would make before starting to cry. Bridget was only halfway back to her room when she heard that cry, that's when she knew there would be no more sleeping.

Bridget turned back around from where she came, approached Brianna and picked her up.

"Brianna, it's too early to be upset." she said with a smile, kissed her cheek and set her back down. She looked over at Michelle and continued to smile. She leaned over and gave her a kiss on the cheek as well, but just before she planted it, she whispered in her ear, "and don't think I don't know what you're doing." She tickled Michelle's stomach, resulting in a case of the giggles. Brianna had already retrieved her brush and was back to brushing the hair of her dolls.

Bridget stood back up to her proper level. "Well?" she asked, "breakfast anyone?"

"Pancakes!!" Brianna shouted as she let go of her toys to jump in the air.

"Yeah, pancakes!!" Michelle pitched in.

"I'll see what I can do." Bridget said as she walked out of the living room and into the kitchen. It was the room she had walked through earlier when there was an argument to dispute. It existed between her bedroom and the living room, which went on to the girls rooms. They each had their own, side by side.

She began to check and see if they had the necessary ingredients to make the pancakes. Everything was there, there were even some chocolate chips. She would surprise the girls with that. She listened to them as they played in the living room. Every now and then she'd poke her head in there to see what they were doing. The rest of the morning didn't have any more arguments. It was one of the last peaceful moments had in that house. When the bad things happened, they happened fast.

After breakfast was made she went into the living room to inform the girls. She also gave instructions for Michelle to retrieve her father, which she did. Seven minutes later, they were all sitting at the table eating chocolate chip pancakes. When those were all gone, Chris went back outside to continue his work on the yard., while Bridgett got the girls dressed. They would be going around town, there were a few errands that needed to be taken care of. It took all of an hour to do that, which wasn't a bad time for them. They said their goodbyes to their father, he said his goodbyes to them. Chris watched them drive away, and then he carried on with the yard.

3

Just after noon Chris decided he had done enough work to earn himself a break, so he took one. He entered the back door of the house which led into the kitchen, took off his shoes, got a glass and poured himself some water. It was refreshing, it felt so good that he had to have another. It wasn't a terribly hot day out, but it was definitely warm. He grabbed a loaf of bread off of the counter and opened the fridge to see what he could turn into a sandwich. There was lots of ham, it's what they had for supper the previous night. He saw some cheese, lettuce and tomatoes as well, he reached in and grabbed the mayo. His plans for lunch were all figured out. He opened the drawer where the utensils were kept, he was looking for a butter knife, but there were only forks and spoons. He looked where the steak knives were kept and those were gone too. That's where his search ended, he made the assumption that they were all dirty and took out a spoon instead. He opened the jar of mayo, and used the spoon to dig some out and spread over two slices of bread. One minute and thirty five seconds later, his sandwich was complete. He took a moment to admire his beautiful creation. It was a wonderful looking sandwich.

He took it over to the table and sat down to eat. There was a newspaper there, he assumed his wife had picked it up sometime that morning, but she didn't. He opened it, and began to read. He hadn't got past the first sentence when he felt the first tug on the newspaper, it wasn't hard, but it was there. Chris looked up. There was nothing.

Chris was a logical thinking man, he didn't believe in ghosts. That was the moment that put the first drop of doubt in his beliefs. He watched the empty room for a moment. Nothing happened. He was beginning to convince himself that he had imagined it. He had no problems lying to himself. He put his eyes back on the paper and continued to read. He got about as far is he got the first time when it happened again. This time it was a harder tug. Hard enough that it ripped out of his hands and landed on the ground two meters in front of him. The pages began to turn on their own, Chris blamed it on the wind, he didn't check to see if any windows or doors where open, he didn't want to be proven wrong. The pages stopped, they turned forward five pages more, and then back three. Chris watched in shock, even if there was a open window, the draft wouldn't cause the pages to turn like that. He was frightened, he needed a logical explanation, but the only logical thing he could think of was to question what he believed in.

He got up and walked over to the newspaper, he wanted to see what page it had opened itself too. The first thing he noticed was the date. It was wrong, it was a day that hadn't happened yet. He read the words massacre and saw a picture of a house with a striking resemblance to his own house. The only difference was, the house in the picture was burned to the ground. A girl began to climb out of the rubble in the picture. It took a moment for her to crawl out and brush herself off, but once she did that, she began running, she was running towards him with a look of anger slapped across her face. It looked like she had plans to jump right out of the picture to attack him. He took a step back and that was all he saw. The newspaper began twist and crumple, another thing that the wind couldn't do. He thought he heard a tiny shriek as the paper crumpled itself up into a little ball that continued to get smaller until it was nothing.

Chris had zero explanations for what had just happened. The best thing he could think of doing was to try and forget about it. But he could only do that for so long. Especially when the other things would begin to happen, but they hadn't happened yet. So Chris placed this moment in the wastebasket of his mind, hoping for it to be forgotten, knowing that it never would.

Chris kept his mouth shut about that whole situation when the girls got home. He thought of talking to his wife about it, but that would probably just scare her. She scared easy and probably wouldn't want to go back into the house. They had a financial situation that had them tied down to the house. Moving wasn't necessarily a good option. He left the situation alone, maybe he would tell her sometime, just not this time. It didn't matter though, in a short while they would all have a story of their own to tell about the house. And some of them didn't have a whole lot of time to share these stories. He didn't want to do that, but whether or not he told them about what happened, it wouldn't change the events destined to take place.

Chris thought about what he would do when the girls got back, whether or not he should tell them what had happened. His wife might just think he was joking, she scared easy and he enjoyed scaring her from time to time. The girls didn't need to know anything, if he did tell them, there would be nothing but nightmares. It was these reasons that led him to making his decision of keeping today's occurrence to himself. It was just something they didn't need to know about. The house, however, thought different, and luckily for the house, it knew how to talk.

4

A few hours had passed before the girls got back home. Chris was back in the yard when this happened. He began approaching the car as soon as it pulled up. When she opened the door there were several bags in the car with her. He thought he might be a gentleman and assist her with the new investments.

"Wow," Chris said, "you got lots of stuff here." Bridget smiled at him.

"It's all stuff we needed for the house." She said.

"And we got ice cream" Brianna shouted with pure excitement, she still had the remains on her face to prove it.

"Ice cream?" Chris inquired as he glanced at his wife.

"Shhh" Bridget said to Brianna. That's when everybody laughed.

As Chris reached into the car to grab some of the bags he noticed there was a set of kitchen knives in one of them, along with a set of steak and butter knives.

"You bought some knives?" Chris asked, as he thought back to lunchtime.

"Yeah, I don't know what happened to our old ones. They must of got lost somewhere on our travels."

"Lost?" Chris asked.

"Yeah, maybe we lost a box somewhere."

"Is anything else lost?"

"Not anything noticed, other than the knives." she smiled and carried the bags she was holding into the house. Chris grabbed some bags and did the same. He wasn't feeling good. Something wasn't sitting right in his bones. He knew they hadn't lost anything on their travels. He remembered unpacking the kitchen utensils. The knives were there, all of them. He put them away himself. There was something very strange going on, and it was something he had no interest in dealing with.

Later that evening, when all the chores were complete and they were all fed, they sat in the living room watching television. It was a clear picture, they were watching a sitcom. The canned laughter from the television was mirrored by them as they sat around enjoying their evening together. Another joke was told just before it went into a commercial break.

"Can we have some popcorn dad?" Michelle asked.

"That's a great idea." Chris said, "What do you think?" he asked Brianna.

"Popcorn!" she shouted with joy.

"What do you think mom?" he asked Bridget.

"I think that's a swell idea." she said.

"Perfect." Chris got up and went into the kitchen.

"I just have to run to the washroom." Bridget said as she got up and left the room. The girls sat and watched the commercials for a moment. Then Michelle got up, she wanted to get a doll from her bedroom. Brianna sat alone and watched the commercials.

An advertisement came on that caught her eye. It was for an easy bake oven. She had heard of them before, but never got a chance to see one. It was really cool. There was a girl using it, she looked older than her, but Brianna didn't think that would matter. The voice narrating the commercial was a calm and soothing voice. It began to describe all of the cool things that the oven could do, and then it began to speak to her.

"Hello Brianna," it said, "do you like this?"

"Yeah," she said as she nodded her head.

"Yes, of course you do. And you've been a good girl, you deserve it, don't you." Brianna smiled, "this could all be yours Brianna, all of this and everything you ever wanted, do you want it?"

"Yeah," Brianna said with a smile bigger than before.

"Yes, all you have to do is be a good girl, do you know what a good girl does?"

"Umm, she bees good?" Brianna asked.

"Yes, she bees good," the voice on the television agreed with her, "but more importantly she does what she's told." This was followed by some static interference, a few wavy lines and then back to the regular television broadcast.

Chris came back into the living room with a bowl of popcorn. There was a smile on his daughter's face that he admired. He smiled to as he approached his spot on the couch and sat down as he had before. Moments later his wife was back from the washroom and Michelle had returned with her doll. The family was together, and the family was happy.

Chris and Bridget tucked the girls into bed when the program was over, Brianna had already fallen asleep and needed to be carried, but that was all right, it wasn't a problem for Chris. He knew his children would only be small for so long. These were the moments he enjoyed. Michelle was asleep as soon as her head hit the pillow. After that Chris and Bridget went to bed themselves.

It took a while before Chris fell asleep. He kept hearing strange noises. They were mostly creaks in the house that could have easily been determined as a factor of the wind. The thoughts of what had happened during the day were keeping him awake. He tossed and turned for a while, eventually he was able to fall asleep. As soon as that happened, the sound of a chair rocking was heard in the living room. Chris didn't get a chance to hear that though. It was Michelle who heard that. It's also what woke her up. The chair rocked for a while, Michelle stayed awake and listened the whole time. It did eventually come to a stop. She heard somebody walking around after that. They had gone into the kitchen, she could hear drawers opening and dishes getting tossed around. When the commotion in the kitchen ceased to exist, the footsteps made their way in her direction.

Michelle took hold of her blanket and tucked herself under. She was terribly frightened. She wanted to scream, but was afraid to do that. Sure, her parents could save her, but there was something standing between them right now. What if it got to her before they even had a chance to wake up. The footsteps came to a rest, it sounded like they had stopped just outside her door. There were no more sounds, it was silent, and had been silent for a little while. She convinced herself that it had all been her imagination. Slowly she began to peel down her covers to have a peek and assure herself that there were no problems.

Her eyes first took sight of the open door. There was a lady standing there, she looked quite old. She was watching her and she was smiling. A giggle was heard behind that smile. Like the lady was laughing at her. Laughing at her for being afraid. Michelle finally was able to let out that scream she was holding in and tucked back under the covers. The scream was a scream unheard. More time had passed, and nothing happened. She calmed down as much as a girl her age could calm down to in a situation such as that. She remained under her covers and listened very carefully. It sounded like there was movement going on in her sister's bedroom. She listened some more, and then the sounds were gone. She thought about going over to see if her sister was all right. It was something she wanted to do, but was held back by pure fear. As she thought of ways to build up the courage to go over there and check it out, enough energy was used to cause Michelle to fall asleep.

5

Brianna woke up to the sun shining through her window. She didn't have good dreams, but she had a good sleep. She crawled out of bed and went to see if her sister was up. Michelle was fast asleep. She heard some noises coming from the kitchen, she assumed it was her father, he was the only other one who would be up at that time. She went into the kitchen to confirm her suspicions. It was her father all right. He was up and dressed ready to do some work around the house, he was just having himself some coffee and a piece of toast.

"Good morning sunshine." Chris said as he gave his daughter a smile.

"Good morning daddy." she said back as she ran and gave him a hug.

"Did you have a good sleep?"

"Yeah."

"You did. That's great, what did you dream about?"

"Ummm, I don't remember."

"Oh, well as long as you slept well."

"What are you doing?"

"I'm just getting some breakfast before I go do some work outside."

Brianna noticed a spoon on the counter with jam on it. She wondered why he was using a spoon to spread the jelly on his toast, but didn't put too much thought into it.

"Good morning." Michelle said as she snuck up behind them.

"Good morning honey." Chris said as he received a hug for the second time that morning.

"Do you want to play" Brianna asked Michelle.

"Okay." Michelle said with nothing but smiles, she had forgotten about the last nights events, thoughts that wouldn't stay lost for long. They ran off towards Brianna's room. Michelle walked in first.

"Wait!," shouted Brianna, "We can't play in there."

"Why not?" Michelle asked as she backed out of the room.

"Because, it's not a room meant for playing."

"But it's your bedroom, who told you that?"

"I don't know her name, but she doesn't like to be talked about, and she doesn't want playing in there." When Brianna said this, it sent shivers down Michelle's spine. She had completely forgotten about how frightened she had become the night before. The lady who was smiling, the lady who was laughing. She suddenly didn't feel like playing in the house anymore.

Chris was beginning to wonder how safe that house was himself. There was definitely something going on. He wondered if anything had happened to anyone else. Surely they would have said something. He figured his wife might have something to say in regards to the subject, when she gets up and attempts to spread some butter onto her toast. Chris decided it would be best to deal with, when the time comes. There were still lots of work to do around the house, and he wanted it done.

Later on that morning while Chris was working outside Bridget, who slept peacefully all night, stayed right where she was, but that only lasted until she was woken up to the sound of bickering children.

"Hey, it's my turn to use the brush."

"Not yet, just let me finish something."

Bridget looked at the clock. It was eleven already. She was actually lucky to have been able to sleep in that late. She laid in bed awhile ignoring the current argument, wondering if they might find a way to neutralize it themselves.

"No!! Give me my brush back!!"

The argument seemed to be escalating. She got out of bed to stop it before it got any worse. She threw on her house coat and walked down the hall. As soon as she entered the living room where the argument had been coming from, the argument had stopped. Brianna's dolls were out there, the brush was there too. There was just no Brianna or Michelle. Out of the corner of her eye she caught sight of the window, and through that window she could see her daughters outside playing with one another, ever so happily.

"GIVE ME MY BRUSH BACK!!!" a voice screamed in the living room. Bridget took a step back. She stood in complete shock. As the toy brush began to move all by itself, with that, Bridget was out the door.

Chris looked up from his current project to see his frantic wife running towards him.

"What's the matter?" he asked, as he put down his tools and approached her.

"The house," she cried, "there's something wrong in the house." Chris didn't say anything, there was nothing he could think of saying. He just took that time to wonder. Wonder what happened inside there just now to make her act the way she was.

"Where are the girls?" He finally asked.

"They're playing over in that field on the other side of the house." she pointed in the direction she was speaking about.

"What happened?"

"I heard them arguing, they were fighting in the living room, but it wasn't them. I got up to go stop them, but when I got there the argument just went away. Nobody was there. I looked out the window and saw the girls, I saw both of them. They were playing together nicely. But her dolls. Brianna's dolls were out there. That's what they had been arguing about. They were arguing about the dolls, and then the brush, it started to move."

"Now hold on. You said you were sleeping when you heard them arguing. Are you sure you heard them in the living room. You said they're playing outside. How do you know you didn't hear them arguing through the window?"

"Chris, it wasn't like that," Bridget said sternly. Chris didn't have to be told though. He already knew something wasn't quite right. It was just a situation he wasn't too fond on dealing with, not yet. "After, when I was still standing in the room, it happened again."

"What did?"

"The arguing, no, it wasn't arguing anymore, there was just one voice, and it yelled at me, it came out of nowhere, like there was a giant speaker in the middle of the room."

Chris thought this might be an appropriate time to tell her about what happened to him, or about the knives, but thought better of it. He didn't want to drive her into complete hysterics.

"Did anything else happen?" he asked.

"No, that was it." She said. Chris thought about it, but he didn't know what to think, "what do you want to do?"

"I want to," she couldn't think of what to do either, "why don't you want to go see it?"

"What do you want me to see?"

"I want you to go check the house and tell me everything is going to be all right. Why aren't you doing that?"

"Because I believe you." He said. She thought about that for a moment. The man she knew wouldn't have been so acceptable in regards to a situation such as this.

"It happened to you too." she accused him.

"Well, no, not like that." Chris said, Bridgett just stared at him, waiting for an explanation.

"It's the knives, we never lost them. I remember unpacking and putting them away, after that they were gone."

"I don't understand what your trying to say."

"I'm saying what your saying. There's something wrong in that house."

"Because of the knives?"

"Yeah."

"What else happened?" she asked.

"That's all." Chris lied.

"That's not it, there's something else." Bridget took a moment to be angry. "When did it happen?"

"The knives?"

"Fuck the knives Chris!" Bridget screamed. Chris watched her for a while. He was trying to figure out if she was going to calm down or not.

"Yesterday I went inside for lunch" Chris began to tell her what happened when he was interrupted.

"I don't even want to know." She said as she began pacing back and forth, that's what she did when she was nervous. Her anger had subsided, and what hadn't gone away was overcome with fear.

"Don't worry about what happened. I've already decided to get us out of here."

"How are you going to do that? We just spent all of our money moving here, for your job. If we move back you lose the new job and all of the money we invested in coming out here."

"Don't worry about that, just understand I'll get it done."

"When?" she asked.

"As soon as possible," he replied, "if things start to get worse I could send you and the girls back to live at your mothers place. I don't think she'll have a problem with that. Then I can work things out here, find a new place." Bridget thought about the scenario presented to her and thought it was fine. She was in fact wanting to do that right now.

"Fine, that works." She was still upset, but not as much. There was a so-called light at the end of the tunnel, "but you better tell me if things get worse."

"You'll probably know before me."

"What about the girls? Do you think anything happened to them?"

"I'm not sure, I thought about asking them, but maybe that would put the thoughts in their minds." Chris said, "I don't think we should tell them."

Bridget agreed with this, and began walking back towards the house. She got halfway there when she stopped and turned back around.

"Chris," she called, he stopped what he was doing and looked up at her, "I don't want to go in there, not right now, not alone. Do you think you could come inside with me? Just so I can get changed."

"Yeah," Chris said, he couldn't say no to her, not even if he wanted to. He put his current project on hold and began walking up towards the house with her.

Chris waited in the living room while Bridget got changed in the bedroom. He looked around the house. There was a certain atmosphere he could feel that he wasn't very fond of. It was a feeling he felt before, but paid no mind to. It didn't make sense, there was just no logic. But now that he had put some thought into it, there was in fact some logic, and it had been there the whole time. The only problem now was, it was the type of logic he didn't want to think about.

Bridget spent all of that day outside the house. She played with the girls, and helped Chris when she could. When it came time for lunch she took a trip up town to grab some burgers. They ate outside on a blanket she laid down outside on the lawn. Anytime there was an opportunity to go anywhere she jumped on it. She didn't understand how she was going to live there for however long they had to stay there. She was almost hoping for things to get worse just so she could have an excuse to move out of there, and live with the girls and her mother. It was something she didn't need to be concerned about though, there was only one more time she stepped inside the house.

The girls had played all that day, both in and outside the house. They didn't have any problems. Chris just worked on what he could to keep his mind from dealing with what had to be dealt with. Later that evening, after Bridget went to town to get supper, Chris had finally convinced her to come inside. The girls hadn't noticed anything peculiar about their mother's behavior. They just thought she was enjoying the outdoors that day.

Bridget sat outside on a little red bench they had placed on the front porch, Chris came out to talk to her.

"You still don't want to come in?" He asked as he sat down and put his arm around her.

"I don't think I can do it." she whispered. She knew the girls were around, she just didn't know where and she didn't want them to know.

"Come on, you'll be fine. You were fine the first few days. Maybe things only happen every few days. If you could figure out the pattern, you could just leave when it's about to happen." Bridgett didn't respond, she wasn't impressed with his attempt at humor. Chris recognized this and backed away from the silly suggestions. "Listen, when it happened to me, I was alone, and so were you, that's what you said. Nothing has happened when we're all in their together." Chris said.

Bridget thought about what Chris said. It made some sense and as long as he was there to protect her, everything should be all right. Finally she decided to come in, Chris helped her up and held her hand.

They sat and watched the television as they had before. It wasn't as comfortable as it had been the night before. The girls seemed to be all right. Neither of the parents were about to say anything about what was going to happen. They didn't want the girls to be afraid of the house. They also didn't want them to think that they were fighting. Her moving out with her mother might look like their marriage was on the rocks, which it wasn't. The main reason they weren't going to say anything though, was because they weren't too sure themselves. Michelle never spoke of her encounters, because she was a big girl now, she understood that big girls don't believe in ghosts. Not the brave ones anyway, and she believed that both her parents and sister believed that she was a brave girl. Michelle didn't want to lose that reputation. Brianna kept her encounters hush hush as well, but that's because she was told to.

Both of the girls fell asleep out there in the living room. When this was realized Chris carried them, one at a time, to their beds. He took Brianna first, when he did this, Bridget stayed and waited with Michelle. When he came back and got Michelle, Bridget came right along with them. She refused to leave his side after that, she didn't want to be alone, not even for a minute. Perhaps over time she could become comfortable there, but it wasn't that time.

Bridget laid in bed with her eyes wide open. She tossed and turned for a long while, she was having troubles finding a comfortable position. All she wanted to do was fall asleep and get the night over with. As long as she could fall asleep before Chris did, she would be all right. She was expecting it to take a long time before that happened though, it did take long, just not as long as she thought it would.

Chris wasn't tossing or turning, but he was still awake. Many heavy thoughts were on his mind. He couldn't understand the situation, which made a difficult task in regards to how he was going to deal with it. He had the new job which required them to live there, at least in that town. He didn't know where else they could go. They had got a really good deal on the house, he was beginning to understand why. Chris laid there and allowed his mind to get buried in thoughts, as Bridgett slipped away into dreams.

Another hour had passed when he himself finally began to drift away into his slumber, it was just at that moment when noises became present in the living room. Chris sat up in the bed and listened. It sounded like a rocking chair, rocking back and forth at a slow steady pace. He looked over at his wife who seemed to be in a peaceful sleep.

The rocking had carried on for another thirty seconds before Chris decided it was time to get up and investigate. He turned on the bedside lamp and looked over at Bridget, she appeared to be asleep. He got out bed and cautiously made his way out of the room. He could still hear the rocking and it was definitely coming from the living room. He poked his head around the corner to see what he would find, but there was nothing to see, and the moment he poked his head in there was the same moment that the rocking sound ceased to exist.

He took a look around the room, but there was nothing to be found. He went and checked on the girls. They were both sound asleep. He walked around to check the doors, and made sure they were locked, along with the windows. Everything appeared to be well.

He began to make his way back to the bedroom, but the moment he stepped away from the living room, the rocking started again. Chris turned back around. It continued to rock. Chris walked back in as the sound carried on. He moved towards where it sounded the loudest. This was the far corner, just over by the window. He walked over there and stood where logically there should have been a chair.

He looked down and began to pay close attention to the spot on the floor he was standing above. There was a tiny movement as if pressure was being applied onto the floor in a rocking fashion. Dust was getting kicked up with it. Chris began to back away. He wasn't sure what to think or do about it. That was when the rocking stopped. He thought he heard a whisper, but couldn't make any words out of it. He stood there for a little while longer, wondering what he should do. When everything remained quiet for the next while, he decided it might be best to just go back to bed, and he did that. He slept well for the next portion of the night. He had a dream he would never remember, which was a good thing. It was a terrible dream, about terrible things, and although he didn't remember any of it, he still dreamt it, and remained in his mind, somewhere. An hour after Chris finally fell asleep, Bridgett was woken up to a much different sound. She could hear what sounded like an animal running circles around the living room. This frightened her badly, she panicked thinking of the girls. Logical thinking led her to believe that perhaps a coyote or some other kind of wild animal had snuck into the house. She nudged Chris but he remained undisturbed. She nudged him again, a little harder this time, calling his name in the process. He stayed asleep, she pushed him for a third time, one decibel away from shouting at him. Chris rolled over and carried on with his slumber. Bridget's level of concern sky rocketed into a level of extremity. This wasn't like him, he never was a sound sleeper, if a pin dropped in a haystack, it would wake him up.

Fear had become her reality. Fear for herself, but mostly fear for her children. She couldn't wait any longer for Chris to assist with the situation. She took a deep breath, swung her legs down so her feet hit the floor, and stood up. The floor was cold on her bare feet, she noticed, but that was the least of her concerns. She began to make her way to the door of the bedroom when all of a sudden, the running had stopped. Bridget froze into place. There was met with silence. Slowly, she began to move forward, but was once again stopped short when she heard a tiny growl, it was like a warning growl, an "I know your there and you can hear me" type of growl.

The running started again, this time it was faster, and it came with a heavy panting. It wasn't running in circles anymore, Bridget could tell by the sound that it had left the living room and was well on its way to see her. Bridget screamed as she jumped back into the bed. She began shaking Chris quite violently, begging him to wake up, but he didn't.

Bridget screamed some more. She curled into a ball tucking herself as close to Chris as she could, using her hands to cover her face. That all happened very quickly. As Bridgett remained curled up the way that she was, she could hear the sounds of the creature in the room now. There was walking, pausing and sniffing. Slowly, she lifted her face from her hands to take a peek.

Aside from everything that was supposed to be in there, the room was empty. The sounds were gone too. Bridget relaxed a bit. She looked over at Chris, who still hadn't moved. Maybe it was all right now, maybe it was over. Certainly she would be calling her mother tomorrow. Chris continued to sleep. She moved away from him a little bit and laid back down with the tiniest sigh of relief.

She wondered if she would be able to fall asleep again after that. A thought she didn't spend too much time on. As soon as she shut her eyes with an attempt to get some sleep, she felt what would have been best described as a hot sloppy breath slither across her neck. It stunk too. If the creature responsible for this feeling of complete discomfort could be seen, she would have seen it jump on the bed and on top of her. Instead she only felt it.

She screamed as this invisible force pounced on to her. Pieces of Bridget began to fly across the room as she was torn open. Scratches appeared all over her body, as her side of the bed was ripped to shreds.

It hurt her a lot, and she continued to scream. That wasn't the worst part though, the worst part was when she felt some teeth on her neck before it broke open. After that things didn't hurt so much anymore. All of the pain just sort of faded away. The fight in her dissipated into nothing. Her breathing turned into thick gurgles on account of the blood that was pouring into her airways. The struggle was over now, her body laid still like that for a moment, while Chris slept. There was a tiny tug on Bridget's leg, then slowly she began dragging away. Her body plopped onto the floor and continued its course. It slid across the room, down the hall and out the front door. A trail of blood went with it.

The main door slammed shut following Bridget's departure. Chris continued to sleep as Michelle bolted up in a serious panic. The slamming of the door stole her from her nightmare. That's when she came to the realization, that nightmares were good, a nightmare is something you can wake up from. How do you wake up from life. She laid back down hoping she wouldn't hear any more noises, preparing to be greatly disappointed. It was a well thought preparation.

In the room next door, where her sister slept, she heard a noise. It wasn't loud, but it was there. Michelle pulled the blankets up over her head. It started with a thump, then there was walking, but it was walking fast, it wasn't walking, it was running, and it was running towards her. She heard it enter the room, and just as quickly as it got in, it stopped right beside her bed. Michelle panicked. A hand reached out and grabbed her through the blanket. It was a tiny hand that grabbed her.

Michelle screamed and tossed the blanket away. Brianna was standing there, she became frightened and began to cry. Michelle's scream had startled the already scared Brianna. When Michelle realized there was no ghost or monster, but it was just her little sister Brianna.

"Brianna?" Michelle said, "What are you doing in here?"

"I got scared." Brianna replied.

"Come up here," Michelle said as she moved over to let her sister in the bed, "did you hear something too?"

"No"

"Did you have a nightmare?"

"No"

"Brianna, what are you afraid of?"

"She's in there, and she won't leave me alone."

"What does she do?"

"She rocks in her chair and she watches me, she says things, but she doesn't really say them. She just puts her words into my mind. It's like I'm thinking what she's saying, but they're not my thoughts."

"What does she make you think?"

"It used to be just stories, they seem like nice ones at first, but then they get scary. Last night was when she started telling me to do things, but they weren't good things. She keeps bringing knives into my room. She wants me to do bad things with them, and if I don't, she says your all going to die."

"What does she want you to do?"

"She wants death, she wants people to die and she wants me to do it."

"Why doesn't she do it herself?"

"She can't do anything outside of the house."

"She told you that last night?"

"Yeah."

"But you didn't?"

"I couldn't, that's why she's in there bugging me, she says that mom is dead," Brianna began to cry, but she still spoke through her tears. "I think she killed mom."

"Maybe we should go check on her."

"We can't, she won't let us through, we have to stay in here."

"Is that what she said."

"Yes," Brianna paused and looked towards the open door, "we can't talk anymore, we have to go to sleep." Brianna wouldn't say another word after that. She just rolled over and closed her eyes.

"Brianna?" Michelle whispered. Brianna wouldn't answer, she just kept her eyes shut tight. "Brianna? Why won't you answer me?"

"Shhh," this sound came from the door way. Michelle was quiet after that. She also thought it would be best if her and her sister tucked themselves under the blanket, which was what they did. Both of them remained awake for what was the remainder of the longest night of their lives. Many unsettling sounds were heard during these hours, and that night lasted a long long time.

6

Chris woke up from his sleep, he looked at the clock, it was one thirty in the morning. He laid back down and rolled over to cuddle his wife. That's when he discovered three things, the bed was covered in what he believed to be blood, the mattress was cut to shreds, and it smelt bad.

Chris reached towards his night stand and turned on his bedside lamp. The light revealed the remains of what looked like a massacre. There were tiny pieces of flesh and bone where his wife usually slept. Blood was splashed all over the room. It was even dripping from parts of the ceiling. He was hoping this was all just a dream, it was something he wasn't interested in dealing with, but here it was, and it felt all too real.

Slowly he got out of the bed and approached the door. There was a trail of blood going that way, he was certain it belonged to his wife. He moved forward with caution. Turning on all the lights along the way. The trail led to the main door, which lead outside through the living room. He tried to open it, but it was locked. He tried to unlock it, but it wouldn't budge. Panic began to run its course through Chris's veins, not a lot, but it was there.

He backed away still staring at the door. He was in complete disbelief. His next thought was the welfare of his children. He turned and ran towards the girls rooms, turning on every light along the way. Brianna's room was first. He ran through the door and turned on the light to reveal an empty bed. He ran in and nudged the blanket, just to see if she had tucked herself in there, but she hadn't. The panic that had entered Chris earlier stepped up a few notches. His next thought was to check in Michelle's room, hoping he would find her there, maybe he would find all of them there.

When he turned around to exit the room, he noticed all of the lights in the rest of the house had been turned off, that's when the door slammed itself shut. He still ran that way to try and open it, with no success. He began to kick it, but nothing was happening, the door was just too strong. He turned towards the window, which was just above Brianna's bed. He flung open the curtains and caught the reflection of an old lady standing directly behind him, she was smiling, with a giant knife in her hand. She had that hand raised up above his head. He turned around to catch her before she brought it down on him, but no one was there. It was just him, and an empty room.

He looked back at the reflection in the window. The room was empty there too. All except for him. He went back towards the window to see if he could open it up, he had his doubts, and when it wouldn't budge, these doubts where confirmed. He hadn't given up hope though, not yet. He picked up the small metal chair Brianna used for her tea parties and launched it at the window. The chair bounced back and nothing happened. That's when he heard some giggles. He turned around to see that the door had opened up, there were two little girls watching him and giggling. They similar, but they weren't his girls. He began to approach them, ever so slowly. They continued to giggle. As he got closer the quieted down, and eventually stopped. Chris wondered if he had frightened them. They turned in opposite directions and ran away, one towards the living room, and the other one into Michelle's. The girl that ran into Michelle's room, made sure to give Chris a wink before she did so. The door had shut itself at the same time they made their departure. He knew it wouldn't open, but he ran for it anyway. He punched and kicked it a few more times with nothing to brag about. He decided he still had a chance to get out, but those chances involved the window. He turned to make another attempt at that, when he noticed there was a lady laying in the bed now. Her face was covered in make-up, there was way too much of it, and it was a sloppy job. She had strands of hair hanging down her face, they were all slimy and grey. She was wearing a dirty nightgown. Her eyes were closed, she appeared to be asleep. Chris hoped she would stay that way.

There was a bang at the door. Chris turned to look but nothing had changed. He turned back to the bed and the lady that was sleeping in it seconds earlier, was now in a seated position with her feet on the floor. She was smiling at him. There was a sick chuckle that escaped from her lips. It sounded like a sewer was running in her throat.

"What are we waiting for?" she asked, there was thick gurgle in her voice as she spoke.

"Where's my family?" Chris shouted, with just a hint of rage in his voice. The lady smiled at him. He noticed her hand was reaching under the blanket. He got nervous, when the hand began to come back out there was a knife that came with it. The lady smiled harder now, this was when her laughter really kicked in. Seconds later she was up and running, with the knife held high. There was no rhythm as she wielded it through the air, just random chaotic swinging. Chris was able to duck the first attack, but not the next one, that one landed in his leg. It dropped him, but it didn't kill him. What killed him was the stab in the heart, which happened right after he was stabbed through his hands and forearms, as he tried to block the attack which still lasted for five more strikes.

The girls were still in Michelle's bed. They heard a lot of noises coming from Brianna's room, but neither one of them was brave enough to look or say anything. They could feel someone in the room the whole time. It was most unpleasant.

At the other end of the house, the left side of the house, where a fire had started all those years ago, began to burn again. The girls weren't aware of it at this point. By the time that happened the fire would be past the living room which was where their exit was. Of course there were the windows, but they were young, they never thought about breaking through the window, and even if they had the windows had no intentions of breaking. So they laid there under the blankets, pretending to sleep.

Michelle was the first one to peak out of the covers. They were hearing odd noises for the longest time, but the sound of the fire was quite different. She knew what it was the sound of, just as she knew the room was heating up.

Michelle could see light flickering on the walls in the hallway from the fire. She turned to Brianna and gave her a shove, another attempted wake up call. Brianna hadn't been sleeping, but she wasn't giving away that impression. Michelle began to panic, but she held it back from its full threat. She couldn't wake her sister up, but that didn't mean she couldn't carry her.

Michelle crawled out of the bed and went to the other side so she could roll Brianna into her arms. When she began to pull her, she noticed Brianna was creating a resistance.

"Brianna, what are you doing? The house is on fire, we have to get out." Michelle shouted. Brianna opened her eyes.

"Be quiet Michelle, your making her angry." Brianna pleaded with her, "just get back into the bed, please, you don't know what you're doing."

"We can't stay here, we'll die." Michelle said, when Brianna didn't move she took hold of her and dragged her out of bed.

"No stop it." Brianna yelled, but Michelle kept on dragging her. She was almost at the door when it was slammed shut in front of them, Brianna was pulled out of her arms and thrown back onto the bed. Michelle screamed and ran for the door. She began to pound on it, but it wasn't moving.

"Shhh." Michelle turned around to face the lady who had been smiling at her the other night. She wasn't smiling now though. She grabbed hold of Michelle and brought her back over to the bed, where she laid her down next to Brianna who was already back to pretend sleep. The lady just stood over and watched them. She seemed rather satisfied.

The fire was getting big and spreading fast. Flames began to make their way through the walls of the room they had become prisoner of. Every time Michelle tried to move the lady would push her back down into place. Brianna wasn't concerned about the fire, she did feared it, but her fear of the lady was much greater. She just wanted to be a good girl and stayed where she was.

There was a new sound now, it was coming from outside. The sound of sirens. It was the fire trucks. This new hope filled Michelle with relief. It must have scared the lady as well, she had disappeared. Now all they had to do now was stay alive. She jumped out of the bed once again and ran towards the window.

Just as she got close enough to have a look out, the lady's reflection appeared. Michelle took a step back as the reflection crawled out and into the room as quickly as a spider would crawl. One second passed and she was standing in front of a screaming Michelle. The lady held out her finger, pressed it against Michelle's lips and shushed her for the last time. Michelle continued to scream, at least she was trying to, but nothing would come out. The lady smiled, picked Michelle up and carried her back to the bed. That's when she realized Brianna was gone and the door was open. Michelle sat up in the bed, hoping help would get there on time. She needed to find her sister, that was the priority. She cautiously crawled out of the bed praying not to get thrown back in. She was left untouched.

She made her way towards the door which still remained open. She was sure it was going to slam shut on her the moment she approached it, but it didn't. She looked out into the hall. The fire was everywhere. That's when she saw Brianna come running out of her room and back into Michelle's. Brianna pushed Michelle in as she re-entered the room, causing her to fall to the floor. She turned around and closed the door. Michelle laid on the floor, looking up at her sister who was looking back down on her. There was a look in Brianna's eyes that frightened Michelle quite a bit, but it wasn't as frightening as the fact that there was a bloody knife her hand.

There were no movements for a short while. Michelle tried to speak to her, she tried to say something, but there was no success. "I'm sorry Michelle," Brianna said as she took a step towards her sister, "she says I have to do this, it's the only way we can all be back together. It'll only hurt for a moment, after that, everything is forever." Michelle crawled a step back every step Brianna took forward. She still tried to speak, but those days were over. She was able to scramble to her feet as Brianna kept up with the regular pace. Michelle took another back step, Brianna took a similar step forward. That's when she held out the knife.

"I love you sister." Brianna said. Michelle would of said the same thing, had she been provided with the opportunity. But before Michelle could even think of a reply that she wouldn't have been able to express, Brianna had begun her attack.

Michelle backed up and ducked to the side, causing her sister to run into the wall, the knife slipped. Brianna managed to hold on, but not before putting a slice into her own hand. It hurt, but it didn't bother her. She ran at her sister again. This time Michelle was making her way for the door, it was shut, but she was able to open it. Just as she did Brianna was on her, she jumped forward pushing

Michelle into the door slamming it back shut. Michelle's fingers slipped into the space between the door and the wall, but was quick enough to pull them out before the door slammed shut and caused whatever type of damage that could be caused in that type of situation, and considering her current luck, that would have been a worst case scenario.

Michelle fell to the floor and rolled on her back. Brianna leaped on top of her with the knife held high. Blood was still dripping off the blade. It had dripped and splashed Michelle's cheek as Brianna held it steady, ready to come crashing down.

Brianna began her strike, Michelle shot her hands up, grabbing hold of Brianna's arms before she could bring the knife any lower. Brianna began to shriek. It was incredibly loud and it was hurting Michelle's ears. She wanted to cover them, but if she let go Brianna would surely put an end to their current little scuffle, and it most certainly wouldn't have ended in her favour. Michelle held on to Brianna's arms and pushed her away. Brianna fell and slid a small ways across the floor. She still held onto the knife.

Brianna wasn't slow to get up. In one hop she was on her feet again, running after Michelle, still making the high pitch squealing. She ran towards the window, Brianna met her halfway, Michelle was already prepared for that. She grabbed her arms again and swung her into the wall. This time the knife did drop. Michelle was quick to grab it. Brianna got up and screamed some more. She ran out of the room and into the flaming hall. Michelle didn't worry about where she was going. She went back to the window and picked up a toy to smash it with. She began hammering at it with zero success.

Moments later Brianna was back at the door, she had another knife in her hand, this time it looked like it was a little bit bigger. She wasn't too sure though, she didn't have enough time to make that comparison, before it was on its way into her direction. Brianna jumped at her sister on the last steps of her sprint across the room. The knife struck Michelle's leg as she backed into the window. She tried to scream, but nothing came out. Brianna pulled the knife from her leg and was about to bring it down again, when Michelle used her good leg to kick her away. That's when the glass from the window behind her shattered. There was a man dressed in fire fighting attire. This frightened Brianna, she dropped her knife and ran to the corner of the room where she curled herself into a ball and began rocking.

The fire fighter carefully pulled Michelle out through the window. She was immediately taken to the back of the ambulance. They wrapped up her leg to stop the bleeding. She would get stitches later on while she was in the hospital. They asked her some questions that she wasn't capable of answering. They figured she was just in shock, and in time would begin to speak to them, they were wrong about that. That's why the story of what happened in that house got altered the way that it did. Evidence gathered from the scene led detectives to a wrong assumption of those nights events.

It took some unnecessary effort to get Brianna out of the house. Once they got her out, she slipped through their arms and tried running back in. They caught her before that could happen and brought her over to the ambulance her sister had been in.

Michelle saw them carrying her towards them. She began to panic, she wasn't sure how her sister would behave, she wasn't even sure if it was her sister at all. Everything happened so suddenly. Michelle tried talking to the medics, but she couldn't say what needed to be said. As her sister got closer she began to panic, she jumped up to get out, but they had a hold of her before she could make an escape. They assumed she was going into some kind of shock. They tried to lay her down, but she was resisting quite well.

One of the medics pulled out a needle. It contained a drug meant to calm a person down. He stuck it in Michelle's arm and pressed in the plunger. Michelle began to relax, she tried to fight it, but with no success. She laid back down as she continued her attempt to fight the sleep, but that wasn't going to happen.

The last thing Michelle saw before the drug took full effect, was her sister laying down bedside her. Brianna watched her, she waited for Michelle to make eye contact. When that happened Brianna smiled, and then she winked. Michelle went to sleep.

7

On that night the house burnt down to the ground, and all the spirits inside the house at the time, burned down right along with it. Michelle never talked again, she became quite depressed on account of the whole situation. She spent the rest of her years staring out windows or at a wall, wherever it was the staff at Landmark Asylum decided to roll her.

Brianna's attitude shifted, she wasn't the cheerful child she had been and never would be again. They shipped her off to foster care in Landmark, where she was picked by a very loving family and raised in the most proper fashion. However, she didn't this loving atmosphere to be completely acceptable. When she got into her teens she discovered torturing animals was an enjoyable past time. When she was old enough to get a job and move on her own she did that. The family was relived.

No one was able to track her down after that, not that anybody wanted to. She didn't go by Brianna anymore, she thought it would be better to switch back to her old name. Margaret, she had grown up to be one of the devils finer children.

Detectives found a ton of evidence back at the house the night of the fire, It all pointed at Michelle, including the statement from Brianna. Her statement said that she was sleeping. When she woke up, the house was on fire and everyone was dead. Her sister had been trying to kill her ever since. The firefighters arrived just in time as she was caught in a battle of self defense. Michelle never bothered to argue the statement, and the cops bought it.

The mother never was found, other than a few pieces that were burnt up in the fire and a few more chunks of flesh scattered in the field at the back of the house.

Years later, where the eighteenth house once stood, a new house was erected. None of the spirits that burned down with the old house ever came back to bother anybody, But the land was still foul, as it always was, and it spread, as it always had, surviving in the shadows of Fernwood.

THE BURGER
SHACK

1

"Stop on by for the finest in flavour!" It was scribbled across the sign posted on the highway leading into Fernwood, just under the heading Burger Shack. It was just another one of the promotions for the new restaurant that were popping up all around town. It was a project that had remained somewhat of a secret until recently which was an accomplishment all on its own considering how difficult it is to hold a secret in any small town, especially Fernwood. Perhaps it had something to do with the fact that it wasn't much of a small town anymore. It had grown quite a bit over the last decade.

Rick watched it grow from the bottom, he had been there his whole life, all the way back to when it was mostly fields. At that time you had to travel 180 kilometres west where the big city was if you needed anything out of the ordinary. Fernwood had always been able to provide the people with life's basic necessities, but if you wanted anything special, the city was the way to go.

Fernwood became a village in 1955, and became a town sixteen years later.

Rick ran and operated an auto mechanic shop that used to be an abandoned saloon back before there ever was a

Fernwood. It used to be a little ways out of town, but as the town grew it got a bit closer, but not too close. His house was there too. Built a short distance behind the shop. Rick enjoyed his privacy. As the town grew he got worried that he might lose it, but as the years passed on he grew less and less concerned. He was sure the town would reach over there someday, when the town grew up to become a city, but that wasn't his time. Rick was an old man.

For fifty years Rick ran that place. Open every day except for Sunday. He was somewhat of a religious man, he kept Sunday for God. Of course if someone was in a serious bind he would be there to help them, that was up until about nine months ago, when he suffered from a fatal heart attack. Rick was seventy five years old.

He had one daughter Christine, who moved out of the town as soon as she could. Like most of the teenagers growing up there she thought it would turn out to be a dead end. When she got the news of her father's death, she flew back and handled everything that needed to be handled. Her mother had passed years ago from cancer. Rick loved her very much and never looked at another woman for love again. So with no one else in the immediate family the shop was of course left to Christine. She didn't know much about cars, so she did the only logical thing she could think of, she sold it.

The sale went through the real-estate agency, so she never met the new owners, and neither did anybody else, with the exception of the broker who took pride in his tight lips.

Immediately after the building was sold, the house being sold with it, tarps were draped all over the shop.

It remained that way for the next eight months, and in those eight months the house remained empty. Almost until everyone forgot about it.

After the eight months had passed, a family had moved in. Nobody got a chance to talk to them, to find anything out, because the family never came into town, they kept well to themselves. This wasn't a problem for the gossip queens, they all jumped to the conclusion of what it was going to be when ads began to pop up in the local paper. Posters began to appear all over town. There was going to be a new burger shack. One day someone had driven past Rick's old shop and the tarps were gone. Many people drove by that day, not because they had business in that direction, but because people talk, and the people that listened wanted to see the ruby red building with a giant neon hamburger shaped sign over top of some bright yellow doors that said the "Burger Shack. The people were excited, the people couldn't wait for it to open. Nobody was sure of when that would be, but you could bet it would be busy when it did.

Emmit knew none of this though, Emmit wasn't from town. He was just a passerby. At least that's what his intentions were. Emmit drove past the sign on the highway and took a long enough glance for it to take hold of his attention. It had potential to be a friendly place Emmit thought, and if it was daytime he would have stopped there for sure, but it wasn't daytime and he was sure it wouldn't be open. He looked at the clock on the radio as it turned from 2:33 to 2:34. He sure was hungry, couldn't remember the last time he ate, it must have been at least twenty four hours. Things had gotten a little bit hectic since then.

His wife Jasmine had been acting strange in the last few months, not being her usual self, they hadn't been married for long, they dated for less than a year before that, but he knew her long enough to know that something wasn't right. It started with her working late. Emmit had no problem with this at first, they were a young couple just getting started in the world and of course they needed the money, the only problem was, the money wasn't coming. She had been working all of these overtime hours and only coming home with her regular pay.

Emmit never questioned her about this, but as the time passed on he could feel a change in the atmosphere between them. He knew she was fucking around, just didn't know who with, and when it came down to it, he really didn't care who it was she was cheating with, after all it wasn't that particular persons responsibility to be loyal, it was her responsibility, and hers alone.

Another sign popped up in the distance, he couldn't make out the words quite yet, but from the design he could tell it was another Burger Shack promotion. When he got close enough to read "Burger Shack open 24 hours, 4km." he had decided that he would stop there. It wasn't really his decision alone, if it was up to him he would have kept on driving, he could have driven forever as far as he was concerned. Put all of that chaos as far behind him as he could, but it was his stomach that was troubling him. It had been growling for a while now, Emmit didn't notice though, he was too focused on the events he didn't want to focus on. But so much time had passed between now and his last meal, the emptiness in his stomach became quite painful. It was most likely a wise decision to stop for a rest and something to eat.

He remembered the last time he kissed his wife, the last time he had made sweet sweet love, the only problem was, it wasn't so sweet anymore. The magic was gone. He assumed he wasn't fucking her as good as whoever this new found lover was, maybe it was just one guy, maybe it was a bunch of them, maybe some women too. After all, that's what whores do, and as far as he was concerned that's all that she was. But that wasn't all that she was, she was his wife too.

Emmit began to feel faint as he thought more and more about it, he began to think about his last encounter with Jasmine. It wasn't pretty. He didn't care though, at least that was what he told himself. He believed it too.

Another sign appeared, it read, "Burger Shack, next exit." Emmit turned his blinker on and turned off onto the next exit ramp. It wasn't long until he saw the building. There was a strange atmosphere around it. Something wasn't quite right, he couldn't figure it out though. He never really thought about it at the time, maybe if he had, he wouldn't of stopped there, which in turn would of made his life a hell of a lot easier, but then again, considering his situation, it might not of been.

He pulled into the empty parking lot, for a moment he thought they might of been closed, he remembered the previous sign which said, open twenty four hours. The open sign on the door was turned on, but the lights were all off in the dining area, it appeared as if they were closed. Emmit didn't care, he was there, he was hungry, and he was going to eat.

A bell rang as it was struck when the door opened. Emmit walked in and had a look around. It looked like a very friendly place, or what had potential to be a friendly place had he come at the right time. A place you could take your family, a place where a pee wee hockey team would go to celebrate after a victory, maybe a place two lovers could go on a first date. The last thought turned his stomach and he wondered if he would even be able to hold down whatever he was about to devour. He was sure he could, he hoped he could.

A young woman walked around from the back, she had long blonde hair that would most likely dangle down to the mid section of her back, it was tied up into a bun at the moment. Her eyes were a brilliant blue, you would imagine an angel would have. Her name tag said "Sue," and she was beautiful.

"It's awfully late to be out on a Tuesday night, don't you think?" she asked.

"I'm sorry, are you not open?"

"Sort of, not really. We're just getting ready to open, I mean as a business. We just been getting things ready all this time. So that's why we're closed. You must have read the signs on the highway saying we were a twenty four hour establishment."

"Well yeah, that and how you got the open sign on and an unlocked door."

"Is that thing on?" she looked over and seemed annoyed, "oh that Robert, can't do nothing right, he's my brother, he's here working with us, you see this is a family business. He was playing with them earlier, making sure they were working. Must have left them on. Well, I'll feel guilty now if I don't get you something. I'll turn on the lights in the corner over there, you go grab a seat and I'll be right back to tell you what we have to offer."

"I don't really mean to be any trouble." Emmit said.

"Oh it's no trouble at all," she said as she turned off the open sign and disappeared into the back.

Emmitt walked around to have a look at the place. The lights turned on over by a booth seat in the corner, the type of booth where you wouldn't be noticed if someone came in.

He walked over to the booth and sat down, he was slow, he was thinking, still thinking, there was no stopping that. Shortly after he sat down, the girl came back with a pot of coffee in her hand and a coffee mug in the other. She put down the mug and poured the coffee.

"Your gonna want some of this," she said, "You take any cream or sugar?"

"No," Emmit replied, "black is fine."

"All right, I can get you beef burgers, ain't got no bacon, turkey or egg salad sandwiches, macaroni salad, french fries and battered cod."

"Do you got cheese for the burgers?"

"Of course we do."

"In that case I'll do the cheese with the burger and a few fries if that's all right."

"That's just fine"

"Sue, is it?"

"Why yes sir, that is my name, thank you for noticing." Sue said as she went into the back again, making sure to lock the door. Emmit didn't notice that.

He took a sip of his coffee and had a relaxing moment of silence, he was waiting for that moment. Everything had been so intense for the last while, he didn't even realize how good the coffee actually was. As a matter of fact, if he wasn't so distracted by life, he would have told you that this cup of coffee was the best cup of coffee he had ever had, in his entire life. But instead he zoned out. His thoughts were too heavy. For a moment he thought about fixing things, changing the situation, and just go back. Then he wondered how he would do it. There was no way. Emmit closed his eyes, took a deep breath, and thought about the events that happened not so long ago.

After months of suspicion and minor questioning, which were answered with lies, he decided to do some investigation. Emmit would wake up at seven, every work day morning, he would kiss his wife on the cheek, then go downstairs to make some coffee and toast. This was of course after the morning bathroom rituals, which would put him downstairs in the kitchen at twenty five after seven. He would then get the newspaper which was delivered on the front porch, go back to the kitchen, pour the coffee and retrieve his toast from the toaster. Next he would turn on the little television which rested on the counter in the kitchen. He never had to change the channel, it was always on the news. He would sit, he would read, he would look, he would listen, he would drink and he would eat, all at the same time. This would last until quarter to eight, that's when he would get ready to leave. Depending on the weather conditions, these events could change, but on this day in particular, that's what it was. After that, the routine changed.

Most days he would drive to the corner store, purchase another coffee, a lottery ticket and proceed to work. This day though, he only drove around the block and then he parked.

He parked far enough down the street not to be seen, but close enough to see everything. Emmit waited.

A few hours had passed when he started to think maybe he was wrong, maybe she wasn't lying, maybe she did love him as much as he loved her, maybe even more. He started to feel bad about how he didn't trust her anymore. He thought maybe he should leave, the only problem was he didn't know where to go. He called in sick to work, so he couldn't go there.

Emmit sat and thought about where to go. He didn't think long though. All at once, his new found doubt was thrown out the window, while his original doubt which he had on his wife, was back in full effect.

It was a fancy looking car, and it was turning into his driveway. He watched a young stud of a Negro man get out of the driver side door. It wasn't even two seconds until Jasmine came running out, wrapping her whorish arms around him and pressing her lips to his. He was too far away to be certain, but he was pretty sure she slipped a tongue into his mouth. Emmit felt a hate in his heart, hate for both of them. He watched them disappear into the house. Her giggling like a little whorish school girl.

Emmit started his car and drove it up to the house. He leaned over and opened his glove box where he had tucked away an 1861 Remington. It was old, but the guy who sold it to him showed him that it worked. He fired a couple shots and the man did not lie. He didn't look like the type of guy who would tell a lie anyway. Oliver was his name.

Emmit stared at the gun for a moment, thinking if this was the right thing to do, knowing damn well that it wasn't. He reached over, pulled it out, and tucked it into the front of his trousers. Emmit got out of the car, shut the door and made his way to the house. He turned the handle on the door to the main entrance and just as he suspected, it was locked. He reached into his pocket and pulled out the keys. It was a little bit difficult due to the rage that had currently overcome his body. He couldn't quite hold it together, tears filled his eyes as the keys spilled out of his hand and onto the ground. He reached down and picked them up. As he got back up he took a deep breath to regain his composure. He thought for a moment. He thought long and hard about what was about to happen, and if that wasn't what he was thinking, that's what it should of been. He was calm now. He knew what he had to do.

He put the key into the lock without a problem this time. He turned it and heard the click of the deadbolt hitting the unlock position. Ever so slowly, he opened the door. He took one step in and listened. He couldn't hear anything, not at first. He was all the way in the house now, he closed the door.

He took a few steps toward the stairs that led up to the bedroom where he and his wife shared their most intimate moments. It was at this point he could hear what was happening. The creaking of the bed springs, the moans of pleasure, and then just like that, the rage was back. Emmit was about to bolt up the stairs, kick in the door and… he wasn't sure after that. That's what stopped him from doing it.

Once again Emmit regained his composure and tip toed up the stairs. He got to the top as the moaning got louder. He wasn't sure if he could handle it, more tears filled his eyes, he was close to crumpling and sobbing like a little bitch, but he didn't. He sure wanted to though.

As he got closer to the room, he passed the photographs on the wall of him and Jasmine. Having so much fun together. The Paris vacation, Christmas of 2012, the picnic where he made his proposal, even the wedding pictures. Emmit wondered what she thought when she brought that man through here, he wondered what the man thought too. It made him sick to his stomach.

When he got to the room, the door was closed, he could hear the sounds. He reached for the door knob and held it for a little while, he wasn't sure if he could do it. Maybe it would be easier to slip on back out and pretend this wasn't happening, pretend it never happened, but there was too much life ahead for him to live, and let this go on. Emmit turned the handle, and slowly pushed open the door, not much, just a bit. Enough for Emmit to take a peek and destroy any thoughts of innocence in regards to the situation.

She was riding him all right. Emmit's rage returned in a flash, it was a bit exhausting going through all these emotions so quickly. He began to panic and took a step back. He took another long deep breath and pondered his next move. His next decision, no matter what it was, it was definitely going to be a life changing event. Not just for him, but for everyone. This was it. This was Emmit's moment. He reached into his pants and retrieved his gun. He took a deep breath and…

"Excuse me sir?" Sue was holding a plate with a cheeseburger and fries, she looked a bit concerned, "are you all right?"

"Oh sorry," Emmit said, "I just sort of zoned out there for a minute."

"You got lots on your mind?" Sue said as she set down the plate in front of him.

"Oh, it's nothing,"

"I have my doubts, can I get you anything else?"

"No, thanks, I should be fine from here."

"All right, just holler if you need anything."

"Thanks."

Sue once again disappeared into the back of the kitchen. Emmit looked at his burger with delight. Maybe it was just because he was hungry, but Emmit was certain that this burger was the best looking burger that he had ever seen. It wasn't just the look though, it had a real nice smell too, unfamiliar yet pleasant at the same time. Emmit took a big bite and sure enough, it was delicious. It was some good meat, probably some top notch Alberta beef, that's where the best beef came from. There was more to it than that though, the sauce on it was spectacular. The party of flavours dancing in his mouth made him completely forget about the thoughts that had been haunting him for a while. A smile even made it to his face.

When he was halfway done, which didn't take long, Sue had come back out to see how he was doing, before she could even make her presence be known, she noticed he had become somewhat of an animal, devouring his meal, almost as if it was his last. Sue could see that everything was fine and decided against bothering him, at least for the moment.

When she came back out seven minutes later, there was nothing but plate.

"Wow," Sue said, "you sure were some type of hungry."

"I didn't think I was," Emmit replied, "but I guess the facts all prove otherwise, and by the way, that burger was delicious, probably the best I ever had."

"Thanks, I'll let the chef know."

"What kind of sauce is that you put on them?"

"I'm afraid I can't tell you, that's a family secret."

"Well, in that case, I wouldn't mind getting the bill, you've been kind enough I don't wanna take up any more of your time."

"I'll be right back."

As Sue walked into the back, Emmit leaned into his seat with a look of complete satisfaction. It reminded him of the days he would have turkey dinner with the family and unbuckle his belt to give his belly some breathing room, while he laid on the couch until he passed out. He was having a difficult time staying seated, and became frightfully aware that it was becoming extremely hard to keep his eyes open. As he struggled with his new found challenge, he felt the room begin to spin. Everything was so hard to do now. He couldn't even speak right. When Sue came back with the bill he tried to talk to her, but he couldn't. It was all mumbles. Sue didn't care though, she wasn't interested in rescuing him, after all that would delete the purpose of putting the drug in his food.

Emmit's head came crashing down onto the table in front of him. The last thing he saw before he took his nap was the shadow of Sue standing above him, and then there was nothing.

2

Earlier that day, while Emmit was still driving, before his hunger got hold of him, Jasmine was sitting in the living room of the home they once shared. Her entire face was bruised, she took quite the beating. Deep inside she felt she deserved it, but not from him though. There were two officers at the house. One of them was upstairs in the bedroom looking at the scene. The other one was down in the living room with her, asking questions, lots of questions, too many questions. Jasmine's head was pounding, she was tired and didn't want to talk anymore. Jasmine hadn't lived in the city her whole life, she moved there just after completing high school. She wanted to get out of her one horse town. So although she had been a good girl as of late, she had built up quite a reputation before that, a rather large criminal record that Emmit was unaware of. What it all came down to, was she didn't like cops and they didn't like her, but when you end up in a situation such as hers, who do you call?

"Where did he go after he beat you?" the officer asked. He was an older man. The name badge on his uniform said Morrison. She didn't need to read it to know that, they knew each other.

"Is that a real question?" Jasmine was annoyed, "how the hell would I know that? I was laying on the floor unfucking conscience, I told you that. I told you everything."

"I'm sorry, what I meant to ask was do you have any idea where he might have gone, a hangout, a mothers place, a girlfriends?" Morrison's ignorance towards her was getting under her skin. There was no response. "I'm sorry, we're just trying to help you here, and these are the questions that need to be asked."

"Well fuck your questions!" Jasmine shouted, "I want you out of my house!" The officer upstairs heard the racket going on, so he decided to come down and see what he could do to assist in neutralizing the situation. Officer Morrison was a good officer though, miles and miles of experience under his belt. His assistance was most likely unnecessary. But he came down the stairs none the less.

"Well I got as much as I can get up there." He said as he came down the stairs. The name on his badge said Leigh. He looked younger than Morrison, a lot younger. Jasmine didn't recognize him. He was pretty green.

"I think I got as much as I'm gonna get out of her as well." Morrison responded as he rose to his feet.

"What's that supposed to mean?" asked Jasmine.

"It means we're leaving," Morrison said. "You clean yourself up and try to have a nice evening."

Jasmine didn't say anything after that, she didn't even watch them leave. Outside of the house as the officers made their way back to the car, Leigh asked, "So what do we do now?"

"We get in the car and wait for something to pop up on the radio. Maybe get something to eat, are you hungry?" asked Morrison.

"Not so much, what about the lady?"

"She's no lady son, she's built herself a bit of a reputation over the years, not much of a trustworthy person you could say. The story she told, there's way too many holes in it. If she wants help from us she's going to have to tell the truth. This is something she's well aware of."

"So we're just gonna leave it? What if he comes back, what if he finishes what he intended to do?"

"Then we catch ourselves a killer and rid society of two misfits at the same time." Morrison said as he got into the car and closed the door. Leigh was a bit surprised with this remark, but he figured Morrison's been around long enough to know what he was doing. Leigh got in the car and they drove away. There was crime to fight, and honest, hard working civilians to protect. Neither one of them spoke to Jasmine again. She was fine with that.

Back in the house, Jasmine was watching the clock, it was the one they got for their wedding. It came from one of Emmit's uncles, she couldn't remember who though, she thought it was one of the ones who had died since. She watched the clock and thought of their wedding. A flood of emotion spilled through her and for the first time she wished she hadn't been such a whore. She wished she could have contributed to the marriage a little bit more, a lot more. She wished she could go back and make good on her commitment to be faithful, loyal and in love until both of them were at an old age. She should have been more thankful towards him, after all he did save her, and without him she still would have been stuck in her old lifestyle. She probably would have been dead by now. She probably would have died right along with her best friend Susie in that car crash. Of course she would have been with her, they were together all the time. And if they didn't die in the car crash, they would of died sometime between then and now, most likely an overdose on something, or maybe even murdered.

Tears filled her eyes. She began to overplay the scene in her head, of what had happened that day. Kevin was fucking her, she was fucking him, and the fucking was good. It was during this activity when she felt as if she was being watched, she turned to look and saw an empty hallway through the crack of the opened door. Was somebody watching? She didn't think so, but she was sure the door had been closed when they started tearing off each others clothes. Through the door she saw into the hall and caught a glimpse of the wedding pictures that hung there. That's when guilt took over, that's when she couldn't do it anymore, so she stopped. Kevin didn't like this, it pissed him off pretty good, and that's when the beating began.

In the distance she could hear the tires of a car screeching away. She didn't understand why those sounds stood out to her. Maybe she was just trying to focus on something other than what she was going through. He beat her, he raped her, and then he was gone. Most likely never to be seen or heard from again.

She thought of the story she told the police. How she was just at home doing some cleaning when there was a knock at the door. She answered it, this man she didn't know, stormed in and began with the assault. If neighbors were consulted, her story would have been toast, as she recalled going outside and jumping into his arms upon his arrival. Like a school girl, a whorish school girl.

She looked at the clock again, more emotions fled through her, this time her concerns were about the welfare of her husband Emmit. It was late, he should have been home by now.

3

A cold splash hit Emmit's face, he slowly awoke. At first he felt well rested, then he remembered about his wife and her lover. Depression began to kick back in, he didn't want to open his eyes, not yet. A delightful smell began to creep into his nose. It was rather pleasurable, he hadn't quite realized he was being strung up by his arms. As more recent thought's re-entered his mind, he recalled driving, and the burger shack, he couldn't remember anything else. "Did I get wasted?" he thought to himself. He really didn't think so, surely he would of remembered drinking, at least when he started.

A second splash hit his face, bringing him into full conscience. He remembered everything, Sue, the coffee, the burger. He opened his eyes. There was a man standing in from of him. He was a clean looking man, very distinguished. He had a full beard that matched the grey of his neatly combed hair. He was wearing a dress shirt with the sleeves rolled up covered in a blood stained apron. He was holding a bucket full of sauce in one hand, and a big brush in the other, he swung that hand out towards Emmit and another splash was applied.

"What, what are you doing?" Emmit frighteningly asked. The man made no response. He just kept on covering him in the sauce. Emmit tried to move, but he was tied up good. His arms held together by the ropes around his wrists which hung of a hook from the top of the ceiling. His legs were tied together with a similar rope wrapped around his ankles. Emmit wiggled anyway.

"You need to settle down my friend, panic will get you nowhere," the man said this with a thick Russian accent.

"What?" Emmit asked, still very much frightened.

"Never mind, I doubt you'll listen anyway, very few people take my advice, I don't understand why, based on the amount of success my life has been, you'd think people would listen, but nobody does, so go ahead, freak the fuck out."

"What are you doing? Who are you?"

"Ah, two questions at once, I like it. Let me start with the second question first. You see, I'm a huge fan of the introduction. It's something I enjoy quite well, especially when it's myself that needs to be introduced." He paused and took a moment to splash more sauce onto Emmit's cold naked body, "I sir am Donald VanLewis, my friends call me Don, some call me sir, but most call me Chef, and what I am doing is basting you with my special and fancy BBQ sauce."

"Why are you doing this?"

"Well you see, here at the burger shack, we take great pride in out flavour." Chef smiled, and left the room. Emmit screamed for him to come back as he made his exit, but was only answered with the closing of the door. Moments later Emmit heard something turn on, there was the sound of something being pumped into the room, "Gas," he thought to himself, "this son of a bitch is gassing me." Emmit took the time he was supposed to take to have his whole life flash before his eyes, to think of absolutely nothing, life took its toll on Emmit.

When he realized he was supposed to be thinking about his whole life, he also came to another realization, he couldn't smell any gas. It was then that he understood the temperature of the room had been increasing. He was sweating, and he was sweating lots. Lots of the sweat was there from being nervous, but most of it was due to the increase in temperature. He figured he was being cooked, he was under the impression that he was tied up in an oven. He thought too much about it though, he was only in a sauna. He eventually passed out and remained that way for quite some time. Not dead, just on his way.

On the outside of the sauna room, there was an empty room, it was a small room with two doors, one, of course leading to the sauna, the other one leading into Chef's office. There was a book shelf that disguised it on the other side, on Chef's side. All full of recipes, taxes, licenses and cook books.

Chef was an older man. He cooked all his life, he's worked in the most high end places, all around the world. He wasn't famous, but he was well known. He took great pride in his work. Everything seemed to be professional, because he was professional, everything except for what he's doing with poor Emmit, that's just a bit fucked up.

Chef was in his office taking care of some paper work. It was about three hours after leaving Emmit in the sauna. There was a knock at the door. Chef looked up. It was his daughter Sue. He took a moment to admire her, his special creation. All grown up. He recalled her younger days, when she was just a little girl, running around, playing in the fields, refusing to come inside for dinner or bedtime. Now here she was, managing the brand new family owned establishment, there was still time for her to fuck up, and he understood that. But she hadn't, not yet, and that's what he put his hopes on. She was something he believed in.

"Are you busy?" Sue asked.

"Always busy darling," he said, as he put his head back down into his paper work, "but never too busy for you," he spoke the rest without looking back up.

"Oh, its okay, I can go."

"No, what is it?"

"I was just wondering about the opening, everyone's getting real excited. Robert's telling us a bunch of lies though. He said we we're opening next Thursday, is it true. Are we?" Sue's excitement grew as she asked.

"You know better than to listen to what Robert says, I told you when the time comes, everyone's gonna be gathered and told at the same time. I told you that, didn't I?"

"Yes dad." Sue dropped her head, along with her excitement. Chef heard the hurt in her voice and looked up as she said that. He saw her sadness and felt terrible.

"I'm sorry sweetheart, I didn't mean to sound angry with you. Cheer up. Hey, how would you like if I take you for ice cream. Just me and you."

"Okay daddy." Sue was smiling again. Sue was like that. She could go through emotions like nothing, like flipping switches. They were easy to flip. That was only a bad thing if you flipped them the wrong way, if you did that…. it was a bad thing.

"Now just let me finish my work here, I'll come get you when I'm done. Probably about," Chef looked at his watch, "forty five minutes, how does that sound?"

"Perfect!"

"Great, I'll see you then." Sue began to leave when she came to a halt as Chef called her back.

"What is it daddy?"

"Tell Robert to come see me."

Eight minutes had passed before Robert made it to the office, Robert knew there was trouble, he could tell by the way Sue's voice was when she told him he wanted to be seen, so Robert took his time getting there.

"You needed to see me?" Robert asked as he poked his head into the office.

"Yes, come in, close the door." Chef said as he put down his pen and paid full attention to his son.

"What's the matter?"

"Two things, First, I got a car out in the parking lot, I imagine the keys are somewhere in the pile of clothes in the back. Get the keys, burn the clothes and get rid of the vehicle."

"Get rid of the vehicle?, how do you want me to do that?"

"Drive it in the river, blow it up, sell it to a bum, give it to a bum, I don't give a shit, just get rid of it."

"Okay, I'm on it," Robert said as he began to leave.

"Hold on," Chef stopped him, "I said there were two things."

"Oh sorry, I thought the clothes and the car were the two things."

"No you didn't"

"I know," Robert admitted.

"What are these rumors I hear you been spreading about the restaurant opening?"

"Ah dad, I'm just doing a little teasing."

"A little teasing," Chef said, "shut the door." Robert shut the door. Five minutes later Robert came out. He had a split lip and a bruise under his right eye, it was on its way to getting darker. He never lied about the opening of the restaurant again.

4

Kevin sat quietly in his 2011 Hyundai Genesis. He was parked at the corner store parking lot right next to the highway. He was ready to leave town, he fucked up, and anger had got the best of him. That didn't really bother him though, what bothered him was that he was sloppy, and that led to trouble.

He meant to kill the bitch, not at first, but after he got to beating her up. There was a point of no return somewhere in that moment, and Kevin was never the type of guy to turn back anyway. Except for now, but that's for different reasons. At this point in time, Kevin's intentions had been to leave her dead, and then leave the city.

At the time he left her, he figured she was dead. He went to take care of anything that needed to be taken care of before he split. The next morning he was ready to go, but there was something bothering him. It was because there was nobody talking about it. She hadn't been discovered yet. That didn't make sense to him because he knew her husband would have come home and found her. He was thinking maybe she survived, and he didn't want that.

He was thinking about going back there, finishing her off. It wasn't his fault she pissed him off. You can't just fuck a man and quit halfway because you're oh so righteous morals kick in. No, he did what was right. He thought about the forty eight hour murder investigations that appeared on the television all the time. One episode stated that the murderers like to return to the crime scene. They get some kind of thrill out of it. That was his problem, all though it wasn't a thrill he was seeking. It was just some conformation, but if he's around there, and detectives are around there looking, they're going to be looking at the people who are looking. Kevin didn't want to be one of those people, but if she wasn't dead, she was going to the cops for sure, and from there she'd point him out. She could finger him, and this time he wouldn't like it. After the beating she took, she would do it in a heartbeat, any logical person would. She may have lacked morals, but she still had logic.

A heartbeat, he should have bashed her brains in, he should have kept on with the beating until her skull caved, that way he would have known for sure.

He thought back to the forty eight hour murder programs. The biggest rule, assuming she was dead, was that he had forty eight hours to get away. Hopefully for the rest of his life, if not, at least for a while, maybe until he was an old man and couldn't do much of anything anymore. Kevin thought for a long time, knowing that either decision he made was getting closer to too late.

5

Jasmine sat on the couch in the living room, she was curled up in her blanket, squeezing her teddy bear. The one that Emmit had got for her. She couldn't sleep, couldn't eat. It had been over twenty four hours since she last saw Emmit, when he left for work. His office had called that morning asking how he was doing, she didn't understand at first, and when they said he had called in sick the day before, it only added to the confusion. She had contacted the R.C.M.P. and explained his disappearance, but they said he hadn't been gone long enough to launch an investigation. They probably thought he left her, based on the encounter not so long ago, the tone in their voice implied that she deserved it, at least that's the way she heard it, Probably because that's how she felt.

It was a terrible feeling. Her face was swollen and bruised, she looked like a complete mess. Her entire body was sore, she felt worse with her guilt though. About how she acted, how she ruined what could have been a perfect marriage.

She ran all types of scenarios through her head, about how and why Emmit just suddenly vanished. He probably thought she didn't care if he was gone, she didn't blame him.

However, the truth was she did care, she wanted him there now more than ever. She hoped he would come in the door right now and have the most perfect excuse as to why he was gone and where he was. She would tell him about what happened. Not what really happened, just the same story she told to the police. He would get upset for her, and come give her a hug. She really needed that hug. The big question was, would she really be able to live the rest of their lives together under the lie? The bigger question was would she really stop.

Tears began to flow down her face, she was looking through the not so old wedding albums now. Wondering where things went wrong, it actually stemmed from where she went wrong, but that was a long long time ago.

She missed him. Now more than ever. Jasmine glanced up at the clock. It was late. She checked her phone for any messages or missed calls, but there was nothing. She spotted one of her previous messages, it was one from Kevin, she deleted it. Then she deleted his number. She forgot she had his number, then hoped he would forget hers. If the cops knew that they knew each other, there'd be so much trouble. But nobody needs that trouble, there's enough trouble as it is. Kevin had already not only deleted her number, but completely destroyed his phone as well. He also wanted to make sure the cops didn't know they knew each other, he wanted his story to add up too.

As Jasmine laid in pain, many thoughts flowed through her mind, but the biggest thoughts, were the thoughts of her husband. Why hadn't she heard from him? She thought about calling back to the police station, but didn't want to go through the embarrassment, the truth was he probably did leave her. But then she thought worse. What if Kevin got him, he could have seen the pictures, he knew what he looked like, and she had met him on this online bang a married broad website. Why did she get off on that? Why was it so thrilling to her? She didn't care anymore, she was done with that. But what if Kevin got to him and strangled him the same way he strangled her, only this time he finished the job. Jasmine picked up the phone and held it for a while, wondering if she should make that call to the cops or not. She decided to call in the morning, if things haven't changed. It wasn't entirely her decision, it was just that before she could make up her mind she had fallen asleep.

Moments later a black Hyundai Genesis slowly drove by, a few minutes later it drove by again, this time stopping and parking just up the street. The engine shut off and all was quiet. Ten minutes later, the driver side door opened up and a dark figure exited with a large black bag in his hand. In this bag was a crow bar, a bottle of chloroform and a rag. He slowly approached the house, staying hidden in the shadows. It was a quiet street on a quiet night, he was certain no one would see him, and he was right.

He approached the house of Emmit and Jasmine. He slid into the fenced back yard where he set his bag down by the sliding glass doors. He reached down, pulled out his crow bar, and with great success got the door open. He was now inside the house.

Kevin was a professional when it came to B&E's, something he had been doing since the tender age of nine years old. He already knew the layout of the house, a common sense he had was scoping his surroundings at all times. This was also related to his thievish childhood. He had no intentions of stealing from the house, it was just second nature for him to notice things like that. All he had planned on doing was nailing the bitch, but as things had turned out, it wasn't all that simple, and now he had to shut her up, so here he was.

Slowly he made his way up the stairs to the bedroom where he was the previous day. The door was open, wide open, he peeked inside, there was still blood everywhere. He could see where there were attempts at cleaning it up, but only attempts. She probably couldn't handle the thoughts going through her head, the memories of him laying down his law. This made Kevin smile. The truth was she couldn't handle the cleaning, not because of the thoughts of Kevin though, it was because she was too concerned with the whereabouts of her husband.

Kevin's smile faded when he came to realize that not only the bed was empty, but the room itself. Where the hell was she? Was she really dead? Was he successful in what he thought he had failed to do, and walked right into the trap he thought he would? No, if that was the case shit would have been tied off, hell, there would have been cops all over the news broadcasts and radios. After all, that's what assisted in making his decision to come back. He had tuned in to the cops radio's and checked all the local news programs for any murders that may have taken place. There were none. Maybe she was at a friend's, maybe they got frightened and went to go stay at the in-laws. Kevin went back down the stairs to get out of there, it was probably best for him to leave. He was on his way out the door, when he caught something out of the corner of his eye.

There on the couch was the bitch he was looking for, curled up with the sweet little bruise he had left for her.

The smile was back now, and there might have even been a little chuckle. Kevin reached back into his bag and pulled out the chloroform. He took out the rag and dumped the appropriate amount into it. Kevin approached Jasmine. She was snoring ever so softly, it was kind of cute. He reached over her mouth and held the rag tight, expecting a struggle which never came. What Kevin didn't know, was he could of dragged her back to the vehicle, stuffed he in the trunk and bumped her head along the ground the whole way there, and she still never would of woke up. Jasmine was a deep sleeper like that, but Kevin didn't know, and even if he did, he was a better safe than sorry kind of guy. So on that night, a drugged up, passed out Jasmine, was carried out of her home, gagged, tied up and stuffed into the trunk of a Hyundai Genesis, without the knowledge of any neighbors. That was the last time Jasmine was ever in that house, or on that street, and nothing could be done about it. Well, Kevin could have done something, but he wouldn't.

One thought briefly crossed his mind, it scared him. He knew there was a husband, but he didn't know where. He found this confusing, but he didn't let it bother him too much. The bitch was in the trunk and they were going on a trip. As a matter of fact, he was turning down the same road Emmit had turned down the day before last on his escape from the city. I guess it was a typical escape route. He got to the highway where he could go north or south. Emmit had gone north, Kevin did the same. It was getting late, he hadn't eaten all day, and he was getting mighty hungry.

6

Late that night, Sue, Robert, Ally and Liz sat in the dining room of their family establishment. Robert was the oldest at 28 he was a huge fan of the practical jokes. Then came Sue, she was 24, and was definitely the most mature one out of the bunch, not the smartest though, far from it. Ally and Liz were 21 year old twins, not identical, but everybody thought so.

They had been waiting for the past eighteen minutes. They were waiting for Chef, he had asked all of them to meet there. Everyone was excited, they thought he was going to be telling them when the burger shack was going to be opening. It was something they all had been waiting for, for a long time. There was minor sibling bickering going on, but nothing serious.

Chef walked in and everything went silent. They watched him as he took a seat at the table they were at.

"Children," Chef said, acknowledging their presence, "I have some unfortunate news, things aren't going quite as well as the planning."

"What does that mean?" asked Robert.

"It means I'm still talking and you need to shut the fuck up." Chef replied. Robert was the only one he talked to like that. It wasn't just because the rest of them were ladies and that's no way to talk to a lady, but it was because Robert liked to fuck around a lot, too much. It got to be a bit of a nuisance. But without his antics he wouldn't be Robert, and without Robert they wouldn't be complete.

"As I was saying," Chef continued, "things aren't moving in the direction they should be moving at the appropriate pace. There has been a delay in the paper work resulting in a push back. I'm afraid we won't be opening for a little while longer, how long that while is remains a mystery to myself, so it shall remain a mystery to everyone." Chef paused as his children began to mumble and grumble. When they realized he was waiting for them to stop, they did, and Chef carried on, "In the meantime, everyone's been doing a great job. I recommend you take the time to relax, cause as soon as these doors open your all going to forget what relaxing means." Robert was still listening to what was being said, but he was more focused on the headlights he spotted coming down the road.

"I'd hate to interrupt, but it looks like a cars headed this way." Robert interrupted. Chef looked over where Robert directed. Robert was right. He looked at the clock. It was 2:53 in the morning.

"All right, everybody in the back. Robert go turn on the open sign and unlock the door." Chef said.

"You know you don't have to explain everything in full dad. You could just say follow the routine. Same thing we did two nights ago." Robert said as he followed the orders given by Chef. Chef gave him a look that said he would be dealt with later. Robert got that look a lot. It was okay though, sometimes the dealings he supposed to be dealt where forgot about. He figured this would be one of them.

So everybody went into the back. Robert turned on the sign and unlocked the door before slipping into the back himself. Once everyone was out of site, the lights were turned low. It looked like they were closed. All except for the open sign. Just under six minutes later, the bell on the door rang.

Sue came out from the back, same routine as before. Except this time rather than dealing with Emmit, who was more a pleasant fellow, she would be dealing with the ignorance of Kevin. He was a wealthy man, and had the attitude to go with it.

"Good evening sir," Sue said, she was about to say more, but was cut off.

"I'll get a table for one." Kevin ordered.

"Actually there's a slight problem, you see we're not entirely open yet."

"What do you mean? Sign says your open, signs on the road say this is a twenty four hour establishment. How are you not open?"

"Well we haven't officially opened yet, we're a new establishment in Fernwood, we don't have all of our papers in orders yet I guess. My brother must have accidentally left that sign on when he was checking it to make sure everything was working fine, looks like it is."

"So you can't get me nothing."

"Well, I feel kind of terrible on account of you coming all this way with expectations of getting some food in your belly. I'll tell you what I can do, I can go on into the back, see what we're capable of making right now, and I'll get right back to you. You can go ahead and have a seat in the corner there. I'll go turn on the light for you." It was the same seat Emmit had been seated at two nights previous. Kevin didn't seem too impressed by what was going on. He didn't like it, but he was hungry, so he sat down.

Moments after Kevin was seated, Sue disappeared to the back. Without the knowledge of Kevin, she managed to shut off the open sign and lock the door before she went back there. It wasn't long until she was back with a mug and a full coffee pot to fill it. She set it down and poured him a cup without asking.

"You take any cream or sugar?" She asked.

"I don't take coffee at all." Kevin responded.

"Well maybe you gotta give it a try, being out on the road this late has gotta put a toll on your wakefulness."

"Just bring me water." Kevin said.

"All right, one water," Sue was becoming quickly annoyed with him, she was thinking about what his near future held and managed to keep up with the smiles, "also we'll be able to make you Burgers, Chicken fingers, french fri-"

"You got chicken burgers?" Kevin interrupted

"No, we got beef burgers"

"Well could you put some chicken fingers on a bun and make it a chicken burger?"

"Yeah, I suppose we could."

"Good then, go do that, I want bacon on it too, with some fries."

"I'm afraid we don't have any bacon." Sue said sadly. Kevin just rolled his eyes, Sue walked away. She never came back out until the food was ready, she didn't forget about the water he wanted. She just chose not to bring it.

In the back she told Robert what he had ordered. Robert lit a cigarette and went to work.

"I don't think he's drinking the coffee." Sue said.

"So what?" Robert asked.

"If he doesn't drink the coffee, he won't drink the drugs."

"Well what does he want?"

"He just wants water."

"Then put it in the water."

"I can't put it in the water, why don't you put it in the food?"

"Why can't you put it in the water?"

"It'll change the colour of the water, he won't drink the water."

"Well for fuck sake, where is it?" Robert asked.

Sue went around the corner and came back with a tiny jar. She handed it to Robert and walked away, but not before giving a smile with a thank you. Robert would of liked to bicker some more with her, before deciding to give in like he did, but he knew she would go to Chef, and then Chef would come to him. He didn't want that.

Three minutes had passed when Robert put up the order. It was done awfully fast.

"Is that even fully cooked?" Sue asked.

"Who cares," Robert responded as he walked away. Sue just rolled her eyes and carried the food out.

When she got to Kevin's table he didn't seem pleased about the water situation. He had been thirsty.

"Did you forget about my water or what?" Kevin asked.

"Oh my, it appears as if I did," Sue said as she set the plate down on the table, "I'll go get that for you right now."

"No, never mind," Kevin said, "I'll just deal with the coffee."

Sue looked into his mug, the coffee was a quarter way down, he was drinking it after all. Then she thought about the drug in his food and wondered what would happen if he took too much. It wasn't that she should of been concerned about, her main concern should of been what happens when you eat semi raw chicken, because that's what was going to be going into him, and chances were, it was going to be coming back out, and the drugs right along with it. Sue went back into the kitchen and waited.

Kevin began his meal. He liked it, it was delicious, and he had never had anything quite like it. After the first bite, he began to go into devour mode. He never even looked at the food he was putting into his mouth, if he had he would have seen clear as day that the chicken was under cooked, but he didn't and he ate it all.

As soon as he was done, Sue came out, almost as if she was on cue. "Wow," Sue said, "someone was hungry."

"You bet sweetheart," Kevin replied, "Lucky for you, I saved room for desert." He said this as he eyed her up and down. Sue didn't like this, but Sue didn't care.

"Will there be anything else?" She asked. Kevin just stared at her, with hungry eyes. Sue walked away. Kevin took a moment to admire her sweet ass. After that things got blurry for Kevin. Something felt wrong with his stomach. He thought he might throw up. He got up to go to the washroom, but lost all of his strength in his legs and sat back down. He began to sweat percussively and at the same time, his eye lids were getting incredibly heavy. The room began to spin, he felt like he was on a helicopter, not in it, but on one of the blades, just spinning and spinning and spinning. Thump! Kevin's head hit the table and it was lights out. Sue had walked around just then. It was perfect timing. As she approached the table, an unexpected event took place. The passed out Kevin began to vomit. It wasn't a pretty sight, it was projecting, and it stunk. Sue called out to Robert. She thought she was calm, but there must of been a hint of urgency in her voice, because Robert came rushing around the corner. Rushing was something Robert never did.

Robert saw the vomit as it was still flying out of Kevin's mouth. His head was getting thrust back with every hurl. It hurt bad for Kevin. If he knew what dying felt like, he would tell you that it felt like this.

"Fuck," Robert shouted as he ran over to assess the situation.

"It was the chicken, you didn't cook it enough." Sue shouted.

"Now's not the time, he's going to puke all that shit up."

"No it's okay, he drank the coffee."

"He drank the coffee?"

"Yeah."

"With the drugs?"

"Yeah, why?"

"I put the drugs in the chicken."

"Okay," Sue said, "Why?"

"Because you said he wasn't drinking the coffee." Robert shouted in a panic.

"He said he wasn't going to, I guess he changed his mind."

"Why did you let him have it, he didn't want it, you take it away."

"I don't see what the big deal is." Sue casually said as Kevin lay puking on the floor. He wasn't puking up as much as he had been, there wasn't much left in him anymore, but he would continue to make the motions and noises up until blood would start to come out. There was a tremendous amount of pain in his chest, there was something bad going on with his lungs.

"The big deal is you double dosed him." Robert shouted.

"So what?"

"So what?!" Robert was screaming now, "you can't double dose"

"Why not?"

All of the commotion brought attention to the rest of the family. Ally and Liz were on their way into the dining area when Chef stopped them and told them to wait back there, while he went to investigate the situation.

"What the hell's going on in here?" Chef growled as he entered the room to find Robert in Sue's face and a black man dying on the floor, "why are you yelling at my daughter, and why is there a man dying on the floor."

"She double dosed him!" Robert shouted at Chef, immediately regretting that decision.

"Are you yelling at me?" Chef asked, with a face that could make you shit your pants. This was when Sue left the room.

"No..Yes, I mean. No, I didn't mean to, I was just in the zone." Robert explained.

"Forget the zone," Chef said, "there is a man, he is dying on my floor, enlighten me on this matter."

"It's like I said, he was double dosed."

"Okay, this man puked up everything he had in his stomach, and ruined my carpet. In a couple of minutes, he's going to be puking blood. Now before he can ruin my establishment anymore than he already has, we need to take him out back." As Chef explained what they were going to be doing, he was rolling the sleeves of his shirt, he knelt down and picked up Kevin's legs, "grab his arms."

Robert did as he was told and they carried him through the kitchen, and out the back door. They set him down behind the dumpster.

"Wait here, watch him," Chef said as he disappeared into the kitchen. He was gone for no more than twenty seconds. Robert watched Kevin suffer, the blood Chef said was going to happen began to happen. Then Chef came back with a butcher's knife in his hand. He didn't say a word. Just walked past Robert and brought it down on Kevin's head. It struck his forehead at an angle, went in about halfway through his head, taking out his left eye in the process. There was no more heaving. It was nothing but blood.

Chef began to dig in the man's pockets. He pulled out a set of keys and threw them towards Robert, they landed by his feet.

"You got a vehicle to get rid of." Chef said. Robert didn't say a word, he just picked up the keys and was on his way. Chef pulled out his knife, it made a wet popping sound as a bit more blood splashed. He took the knife back inside and set it on the counter. Then he grabbed some garbage bags went out back and wrapped up the body. He got a garden hose from the storage shed that was behind the restaurant, hooked that up and hosed down the area. All of the blood, tiny pieces of skull, and bits of brain were washed away for good.

Chef dragged the body back inside. He only struggled a little bit to get it onto the counter. When he did, he unwrapped the body and chopped it into nineteen pieces. He wrapped eighteen of them in saran wrap, and brown butcher paper. They were dated, labeled, placed into a bin, and then into the freezer. The area was cleaned and sanitized ten minutes later. That all happened within the hour. In the next hour, the nineteenth piece of body that belonged to Kevin, was seasoned and placed into the oven, when it was taken out, he ate it. The bones got ground up and disposed of.

Chef was a decent man, but he had an addiction. Addictions are strong and it's incredibly easy for them to win. He grew up in a dangerous part of the world, he survived some terrible things, and that's all anything ever was. It was always about survival.

There was a time, in 1960 during a storm. He was twelve years old, the power went out from the storm, which flooded the whole neighborhood. It stormed hard for a few days. Rescue teams came, but they never found him. He was trapped in the house, just him and his older brother and the family dog. They were hungry, hadn't eaten for quite some time, didn't know how long. Chef woke up one morning and that dog was dead. He didn't know how it happened. His brother said the dog got sick and died while it was asleep. He didn't believe him though, on account of the blood that had been splattered everywhere. He never questioned it. His brother figured since the dog was dead, they might as well eat it. It made sense to him, why let the dog die for nothing, it would give them better chances, and it did. Just not for the whole. When they had the dog, everything was all right, they were full and satisfied. Eventually they ran out of the dog, and still no one had come to save them. It wasn't long until they began to starve again.

When the rescuers finally did arrive Chef was the only one there. He was full and he was satisfied. He was able to dispose of his brothers bones the same way they disposed of the dog's remains. They weren't comfortable with having the dog's bones in the apartment, so they threw them into some rubble from the effects of the flood.

The reason for them being trapped up there for as long as they were, was because when the storm began there was a large tree that was struck by lightning on the side of the road. The tree wasn't big enough to handle it, but it was big enough to cause some serious damage if it fell over, which it did. There was a car, then another car with a large semi behind that. Their parents were in the first car. When the tree fell into the road, the first car slammed its breaks spun and stopped. Next car slammed its breaks and it stopped without turning. The semi did none of this, the semi just kept on going. Went into the second car, which went into the first car and into the tree. Everybody died except for the truck driver, all though he ended up killing himself a couple years after due to depression. The reason he never slowed down was because he wasn't paying attention to the road, he was paying attention to girl who was sucking his dick. When he ran into the second car, her head was jammed down shoving his cock all the way down her throat. When the second car hit the first car and into the tree, the steering wheel smashed into her head for last time. As this happened, her automatic reflex was to lock her jaw shut. She was dead after that. So whether or not he killed himself because he felt so much shame for being responsible for six dead people, or because he no longer had a Johnson, is unknown. It was probably a bit of both. But in the end, everybody died.

Chef was put into foster care, but being the age that he was, living the lifestyle that he was accustomed to, he became a rebel. A rebel with a plan though, there was always a plan. He grew up alone, hunting and scavenging. As he got hungry, he began to get a craving, and when he wasn't hungry anymore, it would still be there.

Crime was bad where he was. There was people getting killed all the time, it wasn't hard to find a body. Little Chef found a way to satisfy his cravings. He was never starved again a day in his life. Eventually, he found a way to make money. He got a job cleaning dishes and bussing tables at a local restaurant. It was at that moment, he knew what he wanted. Of course he still had his addiction, which followed him for the rest of his life.

Robert didn't come back until later, it was much later. Chef never confronted him about anything when he returned. Not because he didn't want to, he was going to, it was just that he had fallen asleep. This was good for Robert, Chef was something he didn't want to deal with right now. Not right now, he had a new secret, and he was trying to find a way to keep it.

7

Martyn was sitting at his desk when he got the news from his superior. At the same time he received the call, he got a bit of a déjà vu. It didn't last long. It was dismissed and forgotten about within seconds due to the conversation, but when it was there, it was uncomfortable.

He was looking forward to this. He always looked forward to inspecting new establishments. He was, of course, a health inspector, working for the government. The papers he needed to sign were one of the papers holding the burger shack back from its launch. Martyn felt the opening of the restaurant needed no delay and was going to have a look to see things over, point out some corrections, sign some papers and be on his way.

He didn't expect to see any major violations. He rarely ever did, and when there was, it was always an honest mistake. They would fix it, he'd inspect it and everything would carry on. Martyn was a very reasonable man. The type of health inspector a food service owner would look forward to seeing. From time to time he would even give advice to certain businesses, which turned out to boost the company's production quite significantly.

He had already done some research on the burger shack project. It was a family run business, run by a not famous but well known Chef. He was scheduled to go there the next day. This happened on the same day Jasmine was abducted from her home. So the day he was scheduled to show up, was the day on the morning when Kevin made his untimely demise.

On that night, the night before the inspection. Martyn had a dream. It wasn't a good dream.

It was night, he was outside, and no one was around. Just a big empty field. He turned around and turned around, but there was nothing. Then he smelled something. It smelled delicious. He turned around again, this time there was a building, he recognized it as the burger shack. It looked empty, it looked closed. But the open sign was on. He began to walk towards it, and then something happened. He wasn't sure what it was, but he couldn't control his body anymore. He tried, but with no success. The weird part was, his body was still moving, and doing the things it wanted to do. So he let it, there was no other choice.

He walked around to the back where there was a storage shed. He opened it up and saw two jerry cans of gasoline. He picked one of them up and began to walk around the building, dumping the gas along the walls. When that can emptied, he went and got the other one. Martyn would try to stop himself from time to time, but he just couldn't do it. With the other can, he carried it to the front of the establishment, opened it up and stuffed in a rag that he pulled out of his pocket. In that same pocket he pulled out a lighter and lit the end of the rag that stuck out of the can. He then opened the door and threw it in. As he tossed it in, he noticed a waitress coming from around the corner, she heard the bell from the door when it opened. She said something, he wasn't sure what. He was more concerned about getting out of the way, which his body did voluntarily. He looked back and watched the building go up in flames. It was burning for a while when he saw the same waitress casually walk through the flames and out the door. She was calm, she looked at him, and then she said what she said again, only this time he could hear it. "It's too late now." were her words.

Something about speaking must have pissed her off, because as soon as those words were out, she was an angry mess. Now she was running towards him. He just stood there. That's when he realized he wasn't being controlled anymore, he had full control of his movements again. He realized just in time. As he dodged her initial attack which sent her sliding behind him, as she passed by he noticed the name on her name tag. It said Sue. When he turned back around to defend himself some more, she had changed. She smiled, then she opened her mouth. She wasn't Sue, not anymore. She had two rows of teeth, each tooth sharper than the last. Two bumps had appeared on her forehead, they appeared to be pimples. As she began to approach him again, with the smile of pure evil, he noticed the bumps were getting bigger. Martyn turned to run, but he couldn't. His legs were staying right where they were. She was getting closer now, and the bumps were getting larger. He was sure they were going to burst at any second and he would get a nice taste of pimple juice. This made him queasy, but he was relieved for a moment when the skin finally broke, revealing two horns. His relief only lasted for that moment.

She grabbed hold of him, Martyn didn't know why, but he felt as if she was about to eat him. She didn't, instead, she began to drag him. He didn't put up much of a fight, mostly because he couldn't, but partly because he was confused, and then he figured it out.

She was dragging him back to building. She had plans on going back inside. Martyn began to scream, Sue began to laugh. He could feel the heat, and it was hurting bad. She dragged him through the doors, everything was in flames. Martyn screamed some more, and those screams continued as he woke up in his bed, drenched in sweat.

He looked around. All was dark around him with the exception of his digital alarm clock. It was showing four o'clock. Martyn laid back down and relaxed. He was all right. He was tired, he wanted sleep, but sleep didn't want him. He laid in his bed wide awake, with thoughts of the burger shack, and how his excitement to go there slowly dwindled down to no excitement at all. As a matter of fact it managed to dwindle lower than that. It dwindled into fear.

8

In the sauna, Emmit held on. There was no tracking time. The sauna wasn't always turned on though, it would go off for a while, and there was light. They would bring him water, they would bring him food. There was no set schedule. Not for the feeding anyway, the sauce they splashed on him was clockwork. He wasn't as frightened anymore. He would doze off for a while, then wake back up. Lucky for him he got to spend most of his time asleep. It was a terrible time. He thought he had become delusional. He woke up most recently and saw his wife, or a woman who looked like her, lying tied up on the floor. Whatever it was, he wasn't too concerned now. He had been there long enough to gain some sort of comfort amongst his surroundings. It was either that comfort or he grew the balls to talk back, he became somewhat of an asshole. Whatever it was that triggered this new attitude, it created an opportunity. An opportunity for him to say all the wrong things, which he did. Just not yet.

9

Robert laid in bed with his eyes closed. He was tired, he was exhausted, he wanted to sleep, it just wasn't happening. Stress was on his mind, it was a chaotic day and there were still some major problems to solve. The events that took place between the time it took for him to leave and come back were borderline nightmarish, but it all worked out. He hoped. That's what was keeping him awake, it was the hope. Robert never had much hope.

Chef told him to get rid of the car, so he did. The last car he got rid of, the one that belonged to Emmit, made its way to a car lot, where some shady guys bought it for some shady prices. Robert knew people, he had connections, or maybe it was just the addiction. The next car was going to the same place, but it was too late out, nobody was available. His idea was to hide it in the woods, then go back and get it later on that morning. People would be awake and he'd be able to deal with the things that had to get dealt. Besides, it was only going to be for a few hours. It was the perfect plan, best he could have come up with anyway. It might have even worked had there not been the unforeseen situation that played a critical role in making his plan the failure that it was. He drove it out into the woods, once he got there he was going to call his sister Ally to come pick him up. She got him last time when he took Emmit's car to the car lot. The car lot was an establishment though. It was easy to take directions to find an establishment. She probably drove past it before, knew where it was before she was even told perhaps. The problem now was, how he was going to tell her where he was, she wasn't good at directions. Not in the woods anyway. She was bound to get lost. After he thought of this, he thought maybe there was another way, and there was. Robert walked.

He got out of the car, closed the door and then he heard a noise. It was a noise that he dismissed due to the fact that he had just closed the door. When he began to walk away and heard the noises for the second time, that's when he became suspicious. He turned back and looked at the car. Sure enough it made the noise again. It was a thumping coming from the trunk. He slowly made his way back to the vehicle and stared at the trunk for a while. There was something in there all right. He could see it moving along with the sounds it made. Not big movements, just little ones, ones you have to pay attention to. This was what he was doing.

Robert thought about what to do. It was far enough out there. He could just leave whatever it was that was in there, in there, just for the night, deal with it the morning. Next he thought better. When he brings it to the lot, whatever is in there, needs to be out of there. Depending on what it was, would make the difference on when he should take care of it, but if he's going to check it out, why not deal with it all at the same time. Now he knew what he was going to do, he was going to open the trunk, see what was making the noise, and assess the situation from there.

He was still staring at the trunk. He hadn't moved an inch, because Robert had another thought.

He had no idea what was waiting in that trunk. He didn't even have anything to defend himself with, other than his muscle, which wasn't that bad. He could fight. Been in lots growing up, lost a few, but not many. As he thought, he also came to the realization that it was going to have to be done. He looked around in the trees and found a branch. It was thick enough to do some damage should it come into contact with anything. It was thick enough to bust open a skull, it was thick enough to be a weapon. He picked it up and made his way back to the trunk. He wasn't worried at all now. He got to the position he felt best, to brace himself for the worst case scenario. He opened the trunk, looked inside and let the branch fall to the ground. It was just a lady, Robert was relieved, it was just a lady. He began to wonder how he was going to get her back. Looked like he was going to have to call his sister after all. He reached into his pants pocket to find his phone. He found it, but he also found a boner. He looked at the lady, and then he thought some more. The lady could see him, she was very much confused. All she knew for sure was that this man was not going to save her, the look he was giving her meant prepare for the worst.

Robert approached the trunk, unbuckling his pants in the process. Jasmine began to panic. Robert liked that, he liked it because he knew he had full control. Robert pulled her out of the trunk and dragged her to the back seat. His hands would be rubbing on his pants any chance they got.

He laid her on her back in the back seat of the car. Her mouth was stuffed and tapped shut, her hands were tied together, and so were her ankles. They were tied well too, better than any knot he's ever tied, or even see his father tie. He wished he could have met the guy who tied her so he could ask how it was done. Then he remembered he already had, and it was too late, unless it was somebody else who tied her up, wishful thinking.

Robert got in the car on top of her. Jasmine fought as much as she could, but she couldn't and she was tiring out. She thought, maybe just sit back and enjoy it, but that was just the old her thinking.

He rubbed on her body some more, his hands were going everywhere. Jasmine didn't like it. Not even a little bit. Robert began to work his way down. When he got to her midsection, he put his face into her belly, gentle rubbing his nose across her belly. She didn't notice his nose though, because this happened the same time that the tongue made its appearance. Jasmine cringed. Robert didn't stop, he went lower. He used the tip of his nose to pull down her sweat pants. It wasn't working well, it didn't take long for him to give up and use his hands. She could feel his breath on her vagina as he brought her pants down lower. She cringed again, but was thankful that it was all that she felt. Robert carried on with his route, all the way down the legs, and then he was stopped. Where her legs were tied together. He couldn't get the pants off. This was a problem, not a huge problem, not yet anyway. Robert, with the boner in his pants and nothing to cut the rope with does what he can and began to untie it. He had to get all the way out of the car to do it. He just dragged her out a bit, so her feet were sticking out. Then he put his head down and focused, because it was tied well. It took him some time, but Robert and his pecker had dedication, and after a brief moment of struggling with the rope, he got it undone. Robert was pleased with himself, his cock was rock hard, he was getting some action, and then he was kicked in the face.

Robert wasn't expecting this and stumbled back farther than he should. He rolled over on the ground. When he looked back up, she was wiggling her way out of the car. By the time he got up and over there, she was out. Her pants were still around her ankles, but she wiggled some more and managed to get herself free of those as well. Robert wasn't too concerned, there wasn't much she could do, her hands were tied up and her mouth was held shut.

Robert approached her, when he was kicked again, directly into nuts. Robert dropped, his boner was gone, and she was getting away. He tried his best to fight the pain, but it hurt, it took him a while to get up, but he did and then he was after her.

Robert was better at moving around in trees, he was more athletic. He was also faster. By the time Robert had got to his feet to give chase. Jasmine had made a good distance, if she looked back, she could still see him though. It was plenty dark, she wasn't sure if he could see her. She guessed he could, because when she did look back he was heading in her direction. It was getting hard for her to run. Not only from exhaustion, but the woods had tricky grounds.

The next step Jasmine took caused her to fall. She quickly rolled into some bushes and stayed perfectly still. Robert who was hot on her trail wasn't so hot anymore. He must not have been able to see her after all, because as she lay in the bushes, she watched him run by at the same speed he carried the entire time. There wasn't even any suspicion. Jasmine stayed quiet in the bush for quite a while. She desperately wanted to get away, she didn't want to fuck this up.

A few minutes passed as she never made a sound. She listened closely for any sounds of movement. When there was none, she raised her hands up as they were tied together, and began removing the tape from her mouth. It took a while, she did it slow, she was trying to be quiet. Her fear was of being heard, but she was more concerned about being able to hear if he was coming back. That way she would know to be silent. It stayed quiet in that area for a little while. Enough time for Jasmine to get all of the tape off her mouth. She tried working on her hands. She figured if she couldn't break the ropes by pulling her hands as hard and far apart as she could, it would at least stretch them, then maybe she could wiggle her way out. This didn't happen though, maybe through time it could of, but time had run out.

She heard him coming back, he wasn't happy, he was mumbling and grumbling to himself. She stayed perfectly still and silent. As he got closer, Jasmine got scared, she began breathing heavy. Panic was kicking in, she took a deep breath and relaxed. She assured herself that he was mad because she got away, he wasn't looking for her anymore. Not in this area anyway. She wondered what he had planned on doing. The distance from her to the car was far, but it wasn't far enough, she didn't think, she couldn't tell. She decided her best option was to stay there and wait. She could see him by the car. He wasn't doing anything, it appeared as if he was waiting too. Eventually Robert got tired or cold, either way he had decided he didn't want to wait outside anymore, and slipped into the car. Jasmine thought this was going to be the most opportune time. She quietly got up, her eyes never leaving the car. Once she was in a walking position, she did just that. One cautious step at a time. When she was far enough away, she ran.

Robert waited in the car. He was upset, he fucked up and was trying his best to understand a way out of the situation. He thought maybe it wouldn't be that bad. She saw him, but it was dark, maybe she wouldn't recognize him. She didn't know where she was or where he came from. He was concerned about the car though. Couldn't have that being found. If they found that it would lead to bigger problems. Robert had all types of little problems. He sat there for another fifteen minutes. That's when Ally pulled up in her car. Robert was tired, he had called her after all. It took her longer then it had too, this wasn't a worry though, he expected her to get lost. Robert got out of the genesis and into the passenger side door of Ally's automobile. He sat down, laid his head back and closed his eyes.

"You still don't want to talk about what happened?" Ally asked. Ally always asked. When Robert called for her to come get him, he wouldn't tell her anything about the situation. It was none of her business and he found it to be a bit embarrassing. But that's not why he didn't want to tell her now, he was just too tired, didn't feel like talking.

"Please, not now Ally." Robert said.

"Fine."

There was a small moment of silence, but it was small.

"Your not gonna give me shit for taking so long?"

"No, I'm just thankful that I have you to count on."

"Awe," Ally was pleased, "that's so sweet of you to say."

"Can I sleep now?"

"Sure."

Ally managed to stay quiet, well as quiet as she could of been. She would hum and sing a few songs from time to time, but not too loud, nothing to wake up Robert.

They got back to their house at the shack. Ally nudged Robert to wake him up.

"We're home sleepy Malone." Ally said, Ally liked to rhyme. Robert woke up, he took a quick look around to realize where he was.

"Thanks," Robert said as he got out of the car.

"Where you going?" Ally asked.

"I'm going to sleep, goodnight"

"Wait," she called, as she got out of the car. Robert stopped and turned around, you could see the tiredness in his eyes, "could you just help me with something real quick?"

"Aww, what is it Ally, can't it wait till tomorrow?" Robert asked as he came back towards the car. Ally had already made it around to the trunk and had it popped open.

"I'm not too sure what to do with her." Ally said, as Robert looked into the trunk, stuffed with a knocked out lady with her hands tied tight together. She was wearing a shirt with panties and no pants. Robert's mouth dropped.

"Ally, why is there a lady with no trousers in the trunk of your car?"

"Do you know her?" Ally asked. Robert nodded his head.

"Yeah, I'm familiar, now explain."

"Well when you called me I could hear the panic in your voice. The panic where you fucked up and I'm the only one who could save you. No clue what the situation was, but I knew it had to be something big. You don't panic like that, not usually. Anyway, I was driving along trying to follow the directions you gave me when all of a sudden this lady was out in the road, with no pants on, waving me down. I pulled over and let her in, she was hysterical. Talking about how she was locked in a trunk for a long ass time, some nigger raped her and put her there. Then she said some other dude was just trying to rape her again, right then and there I knew it had something to do with you. So I punched her in the face."

"In the face?" Robert asked.

"Yeah, I was trying to knock her out, but it didn't work. Confused the shit out of her. Anyway I started smashing her head against her door and she eventually went out." Robert stared at Ally in disbelief as she said this.

"Why didn't you say anything sooner?" He asked.

"You insisted on silence, you didn't want to talk." There was another moment of silence as Robert continued to stare. "So what do you want to do with her?"

"Give me the keys and go back to bed." Robert said. Ally was about to say something when she saw a look in Robert's face that made her think otherwise. She handed him the keys and went to bed. Robert wasn't sure what to do with her, he didn't want to bother Chef, surly he was asleep by now. He didn't want to wake him up with some bad news. He did what he thought was best. He got some rope, and tied the lady back up, just as she was before. She wasn't tied as good though, not even close. He dragged her into the back door of the burger shack, through the kitchen with the freshly sanitized counter, all the way to the room in the back of Chef's office. He laid her on the ground in the corner. The other man was asleep. Neither one of them woke up during the process.

After that Robert went straight to bed, which was where he was right now, but he couldn't sleep.

10

At nine o'clock the next morning the house was alive. Everyone except Robert was awake, Chef didn't care though, he didn't have the time. The health inspector was due to drop in today. He was scheduled for eleven o'clock. As soon as everyone was cleaned and dressed up, they headed over to the shack to make sure everything was in proper order. Robert was supposed to help, but this was forgotten due to the events that took place that early morning. Chef was upset, but everything at the shack seemed to be in good order, so he didn't bother waking him up. He would just talk to him later, there were a few things they needed to talk about.

At eleven o'clock, the family was seated in the dining area. Everything was complete, they were drinking coffee having a friendly family discussion. In the house Robert slept. While Jasmine and Emmit slept in the room at the back of Chefs office. Kevin remained frozen, tucked away in the freezer, while Martyn drove into the parking lot. There were some relaxing moments this day, but not many.

The bell on the door did its thing, and everyone got up to greet Martyn as he entered the building.

"Wow," Martyn said, "this is a beautiful building."

"Thank you, "the Chef said, "it took a lot of work to get here, but were here, and I appreciate your comment."

"And this is your family?" Martyn asked as he looked at the girls.

"Yes, but not my whole family, these are my daughters."

"Ah yes, and very pretty daughters indeed, may I be introduced?"

"Yes, of course," Chef said, as Chef was about to introduce his girls, Martyn was paying attention to them for the first time. One of them looked very familiar. Martyn's blood ran cold, because he wasn't wondering for long. The scariest part was when he read her name tag, "This is Ally, Liz and Sue." Chef got confused when Martyn made no response. A man so talkative doesn't stop talking at a time of introduction. "Are you all right?" Chef asked. Martyn popped back into reality.

"Oh yes, I'm sorry I just," Martyn couldn't think of anything else to say.

"You look a little pale sir," Chef said.

"Yes, I, I wasn't feeling well earlier, I thought I was all right, I just need, I just need a minute, could I trouble you for a glass of water?"

"Yes, not a problem," Chef said as he motioned for one the girls to go get him some. They all got up and left for the kitchen. "Here," Chef said as he pulled over a chair, "take a seat."

"Thank you," Martyn said as he sat down, "sorry about that, I just, sort of got really dizzy, I don't know why." Martyn did know why. He was relieved when Liz came back around with the glass of water, he didn't want to see Sue, he couldn't handle that. Chef took the glass from Liz and handed it to Martyn. He motioned for her to go back into the kitchen, which wasn't necessary, as she was already on her way.

"I hope we won't have to make this happen on another time. We've already suffered from many delays, but if you need to go, it's not a problem." Chef explained.

"No," Martyn immediately replied, "I just needed the seat and the water, in a moment's time, I'll be quite all right, without knowing the fact that this happened, you would never know that it did."

Chef smiled. "Okay, you just stay seated, let me know when you're ready."

"Yes, thank you, it'll be just a moment."

Chef left to the kitchen to talk to the girls, Martyn regained his composure, Robert slept, and Jasmine woke up.

Her mouth was tied shut again, but it wasn't tied good at all, neither were her legs. She didn't realize any of this at first. She was just trying to figure out what was going on. She looked around the room and saw a man with his back to her hanging naked from the ceiling. A pleasant smell was in the room. She tried to speak, to get the man's attention. She began clawing at the tape around her mouth. It was a lousy tape job, it didn't take much time at all. Her legs were tied loose as well, but she hadn't quite noticed that yet. Once she got the tape off she didn't know if she should call for help or not. Who knew where she was, maybe calling for help would have just alerted her kidnapper, or kidnappers. They would come in and do whatever it was they intended on doing. The way the man was strung up frightened her quite well. The most logical thing she could think of doing was assess the situation, and then go from there. She needed some information, the man, assuming he was still alive, had to have some information, hopefully more than her. She decided to wake him. She started to whisper.

Chef came back out into the dining area of the restaurant. Martyn looked like he was doing better, which he was.

"Are we ready to get on with the show?" Chef asked.

"As ready as I'll ever be," Martyn said, as he got back the joyous smile he had on upon the entering of the building.

"Then let us begin." Chef led Martyn into the back of the kitchen, and gave the tour, while Martyn inspected. They started on the main line, where all of the cooking and serving equipment was. There were two convectional ovens with four burners on the top, placed against the wall. Beside that was a flat top, then a broiler. Next were the two deep fryers. Beside that was a door to the walk in freezer. There were only shelves though. If you wanted to walk in, you had to go around to the other side. This was where they placed things for easy access during service hours, such as chicken fingers and french fries.

On the opposite side of this equipment there was a steam table with four large wells. Another tiny flat top and two line coolers on each end. The end across from the oven had two microwaves on a shelf above the cooler. The other end had the same shelf, but this one carried a toaster. The dish pit came after that, with shelving for the pots, pans, and other kitchen equipment. Two staff washrooms were beyond that.

On the other side, when you continued past the main line there was a fairly large prep area. It included a mixer, a meat slicer, two large sinks and one little one for hand washing. The walk in cooler was at the end of the room, and inside that was the walk in freezer, with the shelves you could load up from the inside and retrieve from the other door that connected to the kitchen.

Martyn seemed to be impressed with everything. The food that they did have there was stored properly. All temperature of the coolers and freezer was exactly where they needed to be. It was the product in the freezer that Chef worried about. He was hoping Martyn wouldn't be inspecting their product too much. He opened up the cooler door and looked around. There wasn't much there, wasn't much point to having things that could spoil before you had a chance to use them. The freezer was much fuller though. Things could last frozen for quite some time. Martyn opened the freezer door and had a peek in there. He inspected everything as quickly as possible, it was too cold for him. Everything seemed to be in proper order. He never opened any boxes or looked in any containers, that's why Kevin's body remained undisturbed, while Robert slept.

"Hey," Jasmine whispered. It was a little more than a whisper. Loud enough not to be heard by people she didn't want to hear, but loud enough to get the attention of the man who's attention she wanted. She had been calling him for a little while now, he was either, dead, in a deep sleep or was just choosing to ignore her. She was in hopes on him being a deep sleeper and carried on with the whispered shouting. Maybe she would have to make her way over there. She wiggled her way to a seated position and squirmed across the floor to rest her back on the wall. It was during these movements when she discovered her legs weren't tied as well as they should have been. This worked well in her favour. Using her hands and wiggling technique, she was able to get the rope untied from her ankles, but that took some time.

While Jasmine was working on the ropes wrapped around her ankles, Martyn was completing the inspection of the kitchen and on his way into the dining area. Things were looking very good. He was most certainly impressed. He would stop and write things down from time to time. Chef wondered what he was writing, but paid it little concern, he would find out in time. Anything that was found in error would be rectified and business would begin. The dining area didn't take as long, there wasn't much to inspect out there. Everything seemed to be up to code. Chef's daughters were sitting out there. Martyn tried to appear busier than he actually was, he didn't want to have to speak with them. If he did he would have to speak with Sue too, and no matter how hard he tried, he was still very creeped out by that. Their presence had a lot to do with why he finished that part of the inspection as quickly as he did. Then he was done.

"Well Chef," Martyn said, "everything appears to be in proper order. There are just a few things I need to go over with you if you don't mind, would it be possible to sit in your office?"

"Absolutely," Chef replied, "just follow me."

Chef led Martyn into the other side of the dining room where his office was. They went in and closed the door.

Jasmine had the ropes off now, but she wasn't on her way over to see the man, not yet. She had been lying in awkward positions for quite some time. Her legs had fallen asleep and she was having a difficult time getting them to wake back up. She still had the wall to prop herself against, but so far all of her attempts to get up had failed. It wouldn't be a problem though, not over time.

Robert woke up, he looked over at the clock and saw the time. He laid back down, he found it kind of odd how quiet it was in the house. That's when he remembered. There was an inspection that day. He was supposed to be at the restaurant. There was zero hesitation as Robert jumped out of bed, into some clothes and out the door. He ran across to the Burger Shack and went in through the back door. He walked through the empty kitchen which was as close to sparkling as any kitchen's going to get. There was nobody there though. He walked out and into the dining area where his sisters were. Liz noticed him first.

"Well look who's up." Liz said.

"Where's dad?" Robert asked.

"He's in the office talking to the inspector." Ally answered.

"Fuck," Robert said, mostly to himself, "do you guys know how everything went?"

"I think it was good," Sue said, "they were both smiling when they went in there."

"Well that's good at least." Robert's panic subsided. "I'm hungry, gonna go fire up a deep fryer, anybody want something?"

All of the sisters declined, and Robert went into the back. He walked over to the freezer door and opened it up. There were chicken fingers, fries, shrimp and mozza sticks. He took notice to the chicken fingers and the fries. That's when he closed the door and turned on a deep fryer, he just needed to give it time to heat up.

Jasmine got to her feet, she tried walking and stumbled, she didn't fall though.

"It's good to see everything is in good order," Martyn said as he sat with Chef in the office, "I just need to see what you have planned for your cleaning schedule."

"Ah yes, I have that, it's just out in the kitchen. I remember exactly where I placed it, if you'll be as kind enough to give me a moment I'll be right back" Chef said as he got out of his chair and approached the door.

"Not a problem, I'll just wait here if that's fine."

"That'll be just fine sir." Chef said, but it wasn't. Chef left the room with Martyn all be his lonesome.

When Chef got to the kitchen to get the papers where he knew he left them, they weren't there. That's when he remembered taking them to the house. Rather than going back to tell Martyn the mishap, he chose to run over there and be back a little later than expected. On his way through the back he saw Robert.

"You made it," Chef said as he stopped to acknowledge his existence.

"Sorry dad," I can explain.

"Now's not the time son, we can talk later." Chef began to move again. Robert called out to stop him.

"But dad,"

"Not the time!" Chef shouted as he quickly walked out the back door, turning into a light jog towards the house. Robert gave up on the situation. Chef was getting angry, the last thing Robert wanted to do was make him angry before he was going to tell him something that would most likely piss him off.

In the dining area, the sisters carried on with their conversations. They were talking about times past, all the old memories of growing up. They were talking about how proud they were to become as successful as they had. Sue finished her cup of coffee and realized that none of them had in intentions of going anywhere soon, so she got up, and brewed another pot.

In the office Martyn waited.

Jasmine now had full control of her legs. She walked over to the man, and bumped him with her hands as she called out again. "Hey" she said.

The man wasn't dead. He began to wake. "What? Who is that?" he said, very confused as one usually is upon waking up. Jasmine walked around him to reveal who she was and see what the man looked like.

In the office, Martyn heard a scream, it was loud, but it wasn't a bad scream, it sounded kind of joyous, Martyn dismissed this for the time being, but he was now paying attention, and his focus was entirely on the bookcase.

"What the fuck?" Emmit said as he awoke to the screams of his wife.

"Emmit!!" she shouted with joy, and then remembered to whisper after that, "What's going on here? Where are we?"

"What? How the fuck should I know, I just woke up, what the fuck are you doing here?" Emmit didn't know if he was excited or confused, but he wasn't keeping his voice down.

"Emmit, why are you shouting at me?"

"Why am I shouting? Because this is fucked up, that's why I'm shouting"

"Why are you swearing?" Jasmine was beginning to look sad.

"Because this is fucked up." Emmit saw she was upset, he thought about feeling bad, but then he didn't, "I'm sorry, never mind, just try to get me down."

"Get you down? How?"

"Untie me, lift your hands, use your fingers, fucking untie me"

"Why are we here? And why are you naked?" Jasmine lifted her hands as high as she could, but she couldn't reach his hands, "I can't reach."

"I think there gonna eat us, well at least that's what I think is happening to me."

"Why do you think that?"

"Because they've been marinating me for the last however fuck hours"

"So what do we do?"

"We try and get out of here?"

"How?"

"Go see if you can open the door." Emmit suggested as Jasmine went over there. It was a plunger style handle, the same type of handle you would find on the inside of a walk in cooler. She tried pushing it, she tried throwing her body into it, but it wasn't going to budge.

"I don't think it's going to work. Is there something else you can think of?" she asked.

"Yeah, unfucking tie me!" Emmit shouted. Jasmine looked frightened and a little bit hurt, but she realized that if she wanted to get out of this alive, getting Emmit untied was the most logical thing to do. So she tried, and the harder she tried, the closer she got. She lifted her arms up and then jumped, wrapping them around Emmit's neck. She pulled herself up managed to climb up him and sit on his shoulders while she untied the knot. The sauce that was splashed on Emmit worked out in their favour. It was a sticky substance, which made it easy for her to climb up.

As she reached up and began to work at the untying of the ropes, she got worried. She didn't think she would be able to do it, but as she continued to try, the ropes got loose. The moment she realized she had got it undone, was the same moment she realized, she was about to take a tumble. The fall hurt both of them as they dropped to the floor, but at least they were closer to freedom. Emmit pushed Jasmine off of him and reached down to untie his ankles. After that he would untie his wife. He had just gotten the ropes from around his ankles when someone was heard at the door. Emmit picked up the rope that were around his ankles moments ago and pressed himself up against the wall beside the door. Jasmine got up on her feet and watched.

Martyn had paid close attention to the bookcase. During the time of Emmit and Jasmine's reunion, he actually got up and went over to confirm that the voices he was hearing were infect coming from behind there. It didn't take long before he found the answer. As he inspected the bookcase he gave it a gentle nudge. It moved in a way that bookcases don't move. He played with it some more and discovered a door, so he opened it up. He looked inside. It was an empty room, but there was a door on the other side. He was an inspector of the government, he had every right to go in there. He wondered if maybe they never even knew about it, maybe it was a secret that old Rick the mechanic left behind, back when it was his place. Martyn went into the room and approached the next door.

There were two switches on the side of the door. One was for the lights. He wasn't sure what the other one was for, but it had a timer with it. There was a lock on the door handle, but it was just a small metal pin. Martyn pulled it out, he put his hand on the handle, and then he opened it.

His only instinct was shock. There in front of him was a lady, standing staring back at him. He was about to ask what she was doing, but before that could happen, there was a naked man who jumped out onto his back and wrapped a rope around his neck. Martyn struggled, he tried so hard to escape, but he couldn't pull it off. Martyn slowed down, Martyn dropped, Emmit dropped on top of him, pulling the rope just a little bit harder. It didn't make any difference though, Martyn was dead. Emmit got off of from on top of him and went back over to untie Jasmine, after that he stripped Martyn and put on his clothes.

Chef was in the house, he got the paper, and he was on his way back.

Sue, Ally, and Liz sat at the table pretty much talking about life. There were many stories and jokes that came with the conversation. From when they sat down they had time to reminisce about growing up, and how they became who they are from what they were.

Sue couldn't remember life before her sisters, there was a time though, she could feel it, there were just no memories of it. Robert tried to be bully as much as he could without Chef noticing. They had a mother then too. Not for long, but there was a time. All she remembered was everybody loved each other, not one bad time. None of them could remember what happened, they were all too young. All they remember was that she was there, and then she was gone. Robert would never talk about it, and Chef would always talk about something else, change the subject and drift away. They were home schooled, never left the house much growing up, they went outside when it was time to do chores, sometimes they would play, but they wouldn't leave the property. When they were younger they wanted to, but Chef had told them lots of bad things were out there, he could keep them safe but they had to stay put. Robert didn't believe that though, that's why he chose to leave the property one day.

When Sue was six years old, she and the twins were sitting in the house playing with their dolls. Robert had walked by, he was putting his jacket on.

"Where are you going Robert?" little Ally asked.

"I'm going outside." young Robert replied.

"What you going outside for?" Ally asked next.

"Not that it's any of your business, but the reason I'm going outside is to explore."

"Cool, can I come?"

"No you can't Ally."

"Why not?" this was when Liz jumped in.

"Because I'm leaving the property and its going to be real dangerous, too dangerous for you."

"You can't leave the property!, Daddy says you can't" Sue shouted.

"Well, I am." Robert shouted back, and with that he was out the door. They had all ran over to the window, they watched him leave. They were scared, Chef had told them a lot of the bad things that happened out there. Sue thought it would be best if she got her sisters minds off the subject, so she took them back to play with the dolls. When Chef came home they had told him what happened. He immediately put them all to bed. The next morning Robert was back. He had some real bad bruises, it must have happened from something that was out there, because he never left again. Not without Chef at least. It was all right leaving with him, he could protect them.

That only lasted until they got older. When Robert was in his Twenty's he started to leave. Chef had never said anything and he would come back just fine. He'd tell them there wasn't anything out there and it was safe. The girls didn't believe him, but he insisted.

He managed to get Sue to go out there with him one time, and when she came back, she confirmed the safety of the outside world. After that they started leaving on a regular basis. Chef never said anything about it, and that was that.

They didn't know where Chef worked or what he did when he was out, but he always came back with money or food. All of the siblings took care of the house and that's how everything worked out. There were times when Chef didn't have a job though, those days didn't last for very long, the money got slim, but there was always food.

Somehow Chef had come across a way to make a bunch of money, surely it was illegal, but the only one who knew any better was Chef. The money built up, and Chef built up a bit of a name for himself. Opened up a restaurant, that did well. When Robert got old enough he went and worked there for him. As did the rest of them when they got to that age. By then all of his other employees had quit.

It was funny the way the employees had all left. One of them they all remembered had just up and vanished. His wife had come there looking for him, saying he didn't come home. Chef told her he watched him leave, didn't know where he went after that. Maybe he ran away on account of him losing his job was the only explanation he could give her. Maybe he didn't know how to support the family, so he dodged. The wife didn't buy it, but nothing could be done. As she walked away, Chef grabbed a toothpick off of the table and picked out a piece of meat that had got stuck in his teeth.

Shortly after that, Chef had found the new location, where they were right now. He decided to purchase that land, sell the house and restaurant to start a new place.

The house being so close to the restaurant was what made it so convenient, made life a hell of a lot easier. It took eight months to complete all renovations, Five months to sell the other place and two more months to sell the house, that's when they moved. In the end, everything timed out all right.

That was the last time they were all together. They would have loved to carry on telling their stories, but there would be no more to tell.

Sue looked up in time to see the man come out of Chef's office. He was with some girl she never saw before. Ally knew who she was, but the man she didn't know, Liz knew nothing, but the one thing they all knew was that shit was about to hit the fan, they just didn't know what to do about it. There was a bit of a moment, where everyone just stared at each other, there were no movements by anybody. They were all too scared.

Emmit began to walk, he took a step forward. Sue reacted. Between the two groups of people, there was a server's station. On that station were the necessary things a server would need to maintain their duties when in operation. One of those items happened to be a coffee pot, it was made out of glass, and filled up with a fresh pot of coffee. When Sue passed by this stand, the coffee pot came with her.

Emmit tried to duck, but his timing was way off. Susie threw her arm out, but kept the pot in her hand. The coffee splashed into his face and then to his hands as he brought them up to shield his face. Next Sue meant to smash the pot over his head, but when she brought her arm down to do that, it was held back. Jasmine was there holding onto her arm. So Sue pulled back and put the pot into her face instead. The glass shattered. Some pieces remained stuck in her face as she fell back and bled. This gave Emmit enough time to get up, so he got up and took down Sue. She was putting up a fight, but Emmit had more power, this was when the twins decided to do something.

Liz got up and jumped in, Ally ran to get her brother. Jasmine was in a tremendous amount of pain, but she still wanted to leave. The struggle between Emmit and the sisters gave her enough time to pull the bigger pieces of glass from her face. Then she jumped in, but not before grabbing hold of a steak knife. She swung it in the rumble and cut open Liz's arm, Liz fell down. Jasmine grabbed her, pulled her up and held the knife around her throat.

"Get off of him," Jasmine ordered, as she now had everyone's full attention. Sue let go of Emmit and slowly got up onto her feet. Once she had let go of Emmit, he got to his feet a lot quicker. Jasmine had planned on using Liz as a hostage to make it as far as they had to get, to get away. As she made her move towards the door, Robert had come back with Ally. He had a larger knife in his hands. Ally saw the situation, got frightened and started to cry.

Emmit decided to run. He ran towards the door, which was at the other end of the room, opposite to the both of them. Robert moved after him. Then he heard Ally scream. Robert looked back, Ally was running away, she was headed for the house. Liz was on the floor, holding her throat. There was blood everywhere. Mostly on the floor where Liz was laying and of course, dripping from the knife in Jasmine's hands. Emmit was gone. Robert hadn't realized this, not yet. Sue got up and ran to her sister, she didn't know what to do when she got there, so she just held on to her. Roberts's attention was fixed on Jasmine.

There wasn't much of a stare down between the two of them, and if there was it didn't last long. Robert came at her with the knife. She was able to get out of the way, and as she dodged the knife she was able to come up with an attack of her own. That blow did land, and the same knife that had cut his sisters throat was now sticking out of his arm pit. He dropped his knife, and focused on the pain for a while.

Sue looked at Jasmine, and Jasmine looked at Sue. Robert's knife lay on the ground between them, there for the taking. Then all at once, everybody ran. Sue went for the knife, Jasmine went for the door. It was about seven seconds after Jasmine was out the door, Sue came behind her. Waving the large knife in the air. Screaming a wicked sound. Jasmine ran.

She was running along the road, hoping to be spotted by some traffic. It wasn't happening though. Sue was catching up quick, her only option was to run through some trees, and produce a few obstacles, so that's what she did. Once she entered the trees, she noticed it did slow Sue down. She twisted and turned, she could hear the voice of an angry Sue drift off into the distance. She continued to run, she ran for a while, it took a while before she realized she couldn't hear her anymore. Jasmine looked back, Sue was gone, and it was silent, but the silence didn't mean safe.

As Sue took off after Jasmine. Robert regained his composure. He pulled the knife out of him. This caused a bit more pain, but it wasn't that bad, he was prepared for it. He walked over to see his sister, she was dead. Robert turned around, and that's when the frying pan struck his face. The pan was being held by Emmit, and Robert hadn't gone down, so he struck him again. This time Robert dropped.

Robert was out cold. Emmit put down the pan and began to drag Robert back into the kitchen, where he had come through after he ran out. He planned to sneak back around and claim his revenge. As Emmit dragged Robert's body, Robert remained asleep. He bumped his head as he dragged him up the steps, Robert didn't wake up for that. He hit his head again, as it bumped into the corner of the line cooler as Emmit brought him around that corner, he didn't wake up for that. He set him down by the fryer, opened the door at the bottom where the valve was, and drug his head underneath. Emmit slapped him, he wanted to wake him up, but he didn't wake up for that. Emmit stood back, but before he did that, he opened the valve. Robert woke up for that. The skin on his face would never be there again. He could feel himself melting as he formed a mad scramble to escape. He rolled out from the spray, but it was still splashing on him when he got out, and it was hot. He tried getting up but slipped, and continued to do so three more times before he would just lay on the floor. Robert wasn't dead, but he was in far too much pain to move, so he stayed still.

Emmit walked over, Emmit looked at him, and Emmit didn't care. Emmit was a new man now. The man who went into that sauna, wasn't the man who came out. This man knew when to say he's had enough, he wasn't saying it, but he sure let it show.

Chef came running in next. He looked down at his son lying on the floor. The only thing he could do was to comfort him, but if he did that, then he'd be dead too,

Emmit would see to that. Neither one of them had a weapon in their hands, until Emmit grabbed a fry basket, Chef just rolled up his sleeves.

Ally sat in her room in the house, she was told to wait there until somebody came and got her, so she waited.

In the tree's Jasmine cautiously made her way towards the main road. If she could get there, she could get help. But she didn't know where Sue was, and didn't think she had given up on her, not yet. Jasmine tried to move as quietly as possible. Every noise she heard otherwise chilled her to the bone.

She got to the point where she could see the road between the trees. That's when she started to move faster. She came to a halt when she heard something behind her, but it was just a squirrel running through the trees. Jasmine began to move again, but this time she was at a cautious slower pace. She heard something in the trees to the right of her, but it was just a bird landing for a rest on some branches. She looked back to the road, she was so close. She moved forward some more, she made a good distance, and was being super quiet. Then she heard something to her left, and that was Sue.

In the kitchen, Chef came at Emmit, Emmit swung the basket, it hit Chef in the head, but with no effect. Emmit dropped the basket and took a step back, he would have taken more but Chef had him in his hands and was preventing any further distance. Chef held Emmit as high as he could, and began smashing Emmit's face into his head. He did this three times, then he let him go. Emmit dropped. Chef began to walk away. Emmit knew he was only walking away to get something. Emmit didn't think he would like that something, so he got up, as hard as it was, ran as hard as he could, and threw his body into the back of Chef. This caused Chef's head to snap back, resulting in a minor injury. Both of them were on the floor now.

Emmit spotted a pan on a shelf above the burners. He got up to get it, but he couldn't get far. Chef had got a hold of his leg. Emmit began kicking. This wasn't hurting Chef, but it was loosening his grip. Emmit kicked harder, and began to wiggle. Chef couldn't keep his grip, and Emmit was free. He jumped to his feet, just as Chef had done the same thing. As Emmit got hold of the pan, Chef threw his body into him, the same way Emmit had done to him before. They both tumbled, Emmit with the pan in his hand.

His head bounced off the floor, resulting in the loss of the pan. It travelled a good distance behind them. Chef used his body to pin Emmit down as he began to delivering a series of punches to his face. Emmit couldn't handle it. It wasn't long before he was knocked out. Chef got up and went to get what he had intended on getting before he was taken down by. It just so happened to be a butcher's knife, the same butcher's knife that separated Kevin into all of those pieces not so long ago.

He had the knife in his hand as he looked down on Emmit. He kept that knife there as he walked over, grabbed his shirt collar and began dragging him back to the counter, where he intended to place him. Once he got there he set down his knife. It was within reach which made it a safe location for Chef. He bent down and lifted Emmit on to the table. He eyed up Emmit's throat, where he wanted his knife to land. That's when he picked it back up and raised it high up over his head. He wanted to do this all in one chop, and if he was going to do that he was going to have to come down hard. Half a second before the knife was due to make impact, the distraction in the living room took place.

There was lots of screaming leaving the mouth of Jasmine as Sue dragged her back into the house, there was a trail of blood behind her, lots of it. Sue was angry with her, but didn't know if she should kill her. She would let Chef decide. She didn't want to have any more running though, so she chopped her feet off.

"Robert!!" Sue shouted as she came in. That was the moment Emmit's life got the extension. Chef came around the corner, he paused for a moment. He needed to take the time to be shocked as he saw his daughter all banged up the way that she was. A bloody knife tucked into her pants, a butchered woman in her hands, and a trail of blood that led to who knows where. Chef's instincts kicked in. He knew what needed to be done, now he was going to do it. A lot of attention could get drawn in with that amount of blood lying on the ground, he had to get that cleaned up.

"Give me the girl," Chef said as he approached their location, "take that knife out of your pants, set it down back there, hook up the hose and get all of that blood cleaned up outside, but first lock the doors and shut the blinds. When you're done that, go back and wait at the house with Ally." Sue left without saying a word. That's one of the many things that were so great about her father, he always knew what to do and when to do it.

As Sue made her departure, Chef picked up the still screaming Jasmine and carried her to his office. Eleven minutes later she was tied up the way Emmit was not so long ago. The screaming continued the whole time. Chef came back out to finish dealing with Emmit, he had almost forgotten about that. He bolted to the back where he had left him, Emmit was still there. Chef relaxed, but he didn't slow down. He stood over Emmit and reached towards the empty spot on the counter where his knife was supposed to be, the same moment he realized it wasn't there, was the moment Emmit swung it up, connecting the back end of the knife and Chef's eye. It hurt him bad, but it didn't kill him. His eye had popped immediately, all he could do was hold his hands to his face as fluids poured out, and yell a bunch of bad words. Emmit got up, knife still in hand, and swung it up into Chef's face a second time as he was bent over. This is what put him on the ground, but that's not what killed him. Emmit held the knife high over his head, just as Chef had done with him minutes earlier. The only difference was, Emmit brought the knife down. It struck into his neck, but only went halfway in. Emmit didn't understand the knife the way Chef did. The second chop was the chop that killed him. It was the fourth chop that took his head all the way off.

Emmit got up, and the knife came with him. Everything had turned into a bloody mess, he didn't know who was alive or who was dead. He walked back to the main line in the kitchen, he walked down the line, turning on all of the equipment as he did. He threw a bunch of boxes on top of the burner, then he grabbed a bunch of metal utensils, stuffed them into the microwave turned it on and took a step back. When the fire picked up and the microwave began to produce smoke, he walked away. He made his way out the kitchen, back to the dining area towards the door where he planned on making his exit. There were lots of pops and cracks coming out of the kitchen, he could really feel it heating up.

At this point Emmit was stopped, there was another noise he could hear. It was a terrified scream. He recognized it to. He knew exactly who that scream belonged to. He stared at the office, where his former prison was, the same prison the sounds were coming from. Then he walked away.

11

As Emmit walked out of the burger shack, smoke began to pile out with him. It didn't take long until it was up in flames. Ally watched it happen through her window, Sue was just on her way back to clean up the mess, she saw the flames and came running. Emmit continued towards the road. He didn't see Sue coming. She tackled him to the ground, the knife in his hands went flying towards the trees.

It wasn't hard for Emmit to wrestle her off, that's when he first heard the sirens. Rescuers were on their way. He was relieved. All he had to do, was keep Sue at bay for the next little while. He managed to keep her down as he got up. He delivered some kicks to her in an attempt at intimidation, which seemed to work, Sue stayed down. Emmit ran towards the knife and picked it up, Sue got up again too. She was fixing herself to attack. Emmit swung the knife around, warning her to stay back. It didn't look like she was giving up though. She still wanted one more go around.

The sirens were loud now, the building was in flames, there were no more screams coming from the office. When the fire trucks arrived, they didn't know what to do, on account of the man swinging the knife at that girl in the middle of the parking lot. Emmit began walking towards the trucks, Sue still looked like she had plans on attack. Cops pulled up next, it didn't take long for them to pull out their guns.

"Drop the weapon." Shouted one of the cops, as he stood behind his door, with his pistol drawn. Emmit didn't hesitate, he was safe now, he let it drop. The moment the knife hit the ground, Sue was on him. This startled one of the officers, so he squeezed the trigger. That shot never came close to anyone, just went off into the trees. But the shot did startle his partner, and the partner fired his gun. That bullet went between Emmit's eyes and out the back of his head. Sue was once again covered in blood. She turned back to look at the building. Everything was gone, it was all over.

"Chef?" She began shouting, she needed her dad right now, he would know what to do, because she sure didn't. The cops were yelling at her to get down, but she either didn't hear them, or didn't care. Sue began to run back towards her house, the cops kept their guns in hand and ran after her. She didn't make it very far before they had her tackled and cuffed. They figured from that point it was safe to let the trucks in and put out what was left of the fire. Sue sat in the back of the cop car as they tried to figure out what it was that had gone on there. Most of it remained a mystery for a very long time. Sue wouldn't do any talking, she wouldn't say a word and never did again. The remainder of her years were spent staring at walls in the Landmark asylum.

Five bodies were found in the rubble. It took a while for them to figure out who they all belonged to. In the freezer they found a bunch of body parts, that appeared to all belong to the same person. They were able to run the prints on one of the hands. It had belonged to Kevin Marshal, they were familiar with him. They didn't understand how he ended up like that though. They didn't find anything or anyone in the house.

Their search extended into the trees. What they found there was a lot of blood and a pair of feet. There was no car though. That car was on the highway, and Ally went right along with it.

DIARY OF
A KILLER

1

"I seen my fair share of killing, and I'm ashamed to say I've had my hand in at least half of those. That's just the price you gotta pay when you chose the profession I chose. Sometimes I regret my decision, I mean, sure I saved a lot of lives, helped some people on their way, but when you go to sleep at night, with as much weight as I got on my conscience, well I guess you don't really sleep at all. Don't get me wrong, these were bad people I killed, not one of them was innocent, I can guarantee you that. But what troubles me late at night is the fact that I'm just a man, like any other man.

Who gave me the right to let a man live or die? I guess what I'm trying to say is I'm scared. I'm scared of what's waiting for me when it's my time to answer to the lord. Maybe he had plans with these people, maybe they were intended to change their ways, before I came across them and took that chance away," Andrew took the last drag of the cigarette he was smoking and crushed it in the ash tray on top of the table. He sat across from a much younger looking lady, who went by the name of Wendy. She had a pen and paper, but she wasn't writing, at least not yet. Andrew noticed this, but didn't say anything, maybe he just wasn't saying anything interesting. He knew that wasn't it, he just wasn't saying the things she wanted to hear? "So, you're ashamed of yourself?" Wendy asked," what about all of the lives you saved? Doesn't that mean anything?"

"I don't know, maybe they were the lives that weren't meant to be saved," Andrew replied, "I mean, at this point in time more than half of those lives are dead now anyway. Death, it's the finishing line of the finish line. Everybody gets there, some sooner than others, but it happens, no matter what. It's always there for you at the end.

As of late I got to thinking, and maybe if you could get there quick enough, you could save yourself from all of the sin your life was destined to become involved with."

There was a moment of silence as both of them thought about what Andrew had just said. Wendy picked up her pen. This for some reason relieved Andrew, he couldn't tell you why, but it did. Andrew reached into his breast pocket and pulled out his pack of cigarettes, he popped one out and placed it into his mouth. He held out the pack towards Wendy, in an offering, but she declined. Andrew put the pack back into the pocket he got it from, struck a match and lit his smoke.

"You know what I came here to talk about?" Wendy asked.

"Yes, I suppose I do." said Andrew.

"So where does it start?"

"I reckon it was sometime around 1862, maybe 67, I'm not too sure, that was over fifty years ago, over that amount of time you can't expect an old man like me to remember everything, time has got the best of me.

I had just hired my new deputy. I was catching some serious flack, because that deputy just happened to be a lady. I know it sounds crazy, but it's what it was. All started on account of me putting my foot in my mouth. She wasn't the strongest, the farthest thing from it, but she had an attitude, that's what caught my initial attention. Maybe I was afraid of her, afraid of what an attitude like that could unleash on someone, that someone could have been me, had I not chose to bring her on board. I never would admit that to anyone, not in those days anyway. Now it doesn't really matter, me being so close to the end. At least one could hope so. After you've lived as many years as I have, death becomes something you pray for. Maybe that's why I have a different understanding of things in comparison to my younger days."

"Where does Meloche come in?" Wendy asked.

"Right about now."

2

"ALL ABOARD!!!!" the conductor shouted as the train prepared to depart from its station. Meloche sat in the back seat of the last coach, he had been riding since three towns back, which would have put him on that train for the last forty seven hours. He sat the whole time with not much of an expression on his face. He didn't sleep, didn't use the washroom, didn't eat, just sat. He didn't like to draw attention to himself, it had nothing to do with the fact that he was a wanted man in eight states of America, and two of Canada's provinces, but it was because he wasn't much of a people person. As a matter of fact he hated people. There wasn't one person he ever saw that he didn't think about killing, and there weren't very many people that he thought about killing who were still alive.

"Next town," he thought to himself, "that's where I get off."

Meloche had a reputation, not a good one either, he wasn't the type of person one would approach for any reason, but every so often someone would grow the balls to do it, and if you had good enough reason, then you were safe. If you didn't, you'd be just as dead as the rest of them.

The only risk to that was nobody ever knew what reasonable was with Meloche.

When the man with golden teeth approached him earlier that month, luck had been on his side, and that's all it was. It had nothing to do with the thousand dollars he gave to Meloche to assassinate the mayor of Elks Town, it had nothing to do with the other thousand he was promised when he returned from a completed job. And whether or not he would kill him when he got back was still in the air. Meloche decided he would decide when he got back. Perhaps it was something he didn't have to worry about at all. There were always good chances of him getting killed along the way, but those were only chances.

Meloche closed his eyes and tried to let sleep take a hold of him, of course this wouldn't happen, it never happened. It was the lack of sleep that paid a small contribution as to why he was as loony as he was. So Meloche stayed wide awake, with his eyes closed, for the remainder of the trip.

Five hours later the train pulled up to the station of Elks town. A few other people got off, but not much, most of them were headed further west. Meloche grabbed the bag he had rested under his seat, and made his way off the train. He made it all the way out of the station and up the walkway before he was stopped.

"Good day sir," said a well dressed man. Meloche ignored him and kept on walking, "may I ask how you're doing this fine day?" Meloche didn't respond as the man began to follow him.

"My name's Carl, I'm a proud member of the town council, and on behalf of Elks town I would like to welcome you, may I ask your name good sir?"

"No," Meloche spoke, "but you can tell me where I can find the mayor"

"I certainly can, He just lives up over the hill that way yonder," Carl pointed to a hill, not too far in the distance, "It's a big house, red barn in the yard, huge windows, white structure with a black roof, you can't miss it, may I ask what you wish to speak with him about?, are you here representing Landmark? Is this about the railway expansion?"

"No, I'm not here to speak with him, I'm here to kill him."

"My new friend, that is nothing to make a joke about."

"Well lucky for you, I'm not joking, and lucky for me, I'm not your friend."

"If you're not joking, why would you so willingly admit to what your future actions entail?"

"I'm not known to lie."

"Well what's stopping me from going right now to get the Marshall?"

Meloche pulled out his pistol and stuck it in Carl's face, Carl had just enough time to shit himself before Meloche squeezed the trigger, sending Carl's brains into the dirt. Carl dropped with what would of been no expression left on his face, the only problem was his face was gone.

There were no witnesses to this action and Meloche carried on with his casual walk towards the hill that the late Carl had directed him to. It wasn't long after that when he heard screams behind him. They were coming from a woman who must have found poor Carl. If Meloche ever smiled, this would be the time he would do it, but he didn't.

Moments later the Marshal was on the scene. He asked a few questions, but there wasn't anyone who had the answers.

It wouldn't take long for him to figure it out though. The Marshal was a good Marshal, and anyone who did any wrong in his town would certainly pay the price. That was Marshal Andrew's guarantee.

Andrew looked down at Carl. "Carl was a good man, he never caused trouble for anybody," Andrew said, "why anyone would shoot him is beyond me, he barley had a dollar to his name, anything you could have possibly wanted from him was his personality." Andrew took off his coat, knelt down and laid it over Carl's body, there was a bit of a crowd gathering around, some were crying, some were angry.

"This stuff doesn't happen here," shouted Tony, the town drunk, "not in our town."

"Your right," Andrew said, as he stood back up, "that means there's a stranger amongst us, say, when did the last train roll in?"

"I reckon it was no longer than fifteen minutes ago," Tony replied.

"Right," Andrew thought for a moment, "Gentlemen, I do believe there is a new comer in town, he must not be familiar with Elk town rules and regulations. Justice needs to be served. As of this point I'm making all of you honorary deputies, I want you to spread out, find yourself an unfamiliar face and bring it to me."

A young lady happened to be standing in the crowd. A smile had formed on her face, she was going to be a deputy. It wasn't a big smile, considering the circumstances of the situation, but it was a smile. It was something she had always wanted in life, but never thought it would ever come considering she was female. This moment gave her a light of hope, and hope can go a long way.

"Do you want a smoke?" Tony asked Andrew, as he lit one for himself.

"No Tony," Andrew responded, "I don't smoke, those things will kill you, now everybody, you got your orders, now spread out."

There was what appeared to be some sort of a crowd cheer, but it came across more like a series of grumbles. They began to disperse into their separate directions. When Andrew saw the lady begin to go along with them, he stopped her.

"And just what do you think you're doing?" Andrew asked.

"I'm going to find the man responsible for Carl's death," she said.

"Now I don't think that's a wise idea, maybe you should leave that for the gentlemen."

"I don't see why, you already made me an honorary deputy."

"Oh yeah, and when did I say that?"

"Just a few moments ago, you said we all were, so we could find Carl's killer."

"I'm sorry, what's your name?"

"Its Blake, you should know that, I've lived here all my life."

"I know, it just slip my mind, Listen, I wasn't talking about the ladies"

"You never mentioned that, and it seems a little too late now."

"Do you even have a pistol?" Andrew asked.

"No, but I can fight, and if you give me one of yours I can shoot. My daddy taught me before he passed away five years ago."

"Do you really think you can fight in that pretty little dress?"

"I don't have to wear no dress, I can wear pants if that's what I got to do."

Andrew began to laugh, "Really, a lady in pants, isn't that something?"

"You're not going to stop me."

"Well with an attitude like that, I reckon I wouldn't."

"So why are we wasting our time talking all this nonsense, we got work to do."

Andrew realized they were wasting time, and there was a killer to be caught. He might as well just let her be deputy for the while. After all, he had half a dozen other men already on the job, even if one of them was a drunk. Andrew figured she wouldn't even get a chance to come across the killer, even if she did she would probably tuck her head and run. He was wrong on both parts.

"All right," said Andrew, "but you go home and find some pants first, can't be running around in that dress."

"Yes, right away sir." Blake said, and then she was off, running home to change, running over towards the hill where she lived two houses away from the Mayor. Andrew left in the other direction towards the saloon. He figured after a long day of travelling, one would want to wet his whistle and what better place to stop than the saloon. He was wrong for the second time that day.

3

As the Marshal and Blake were trading words, Mayor Douglas sat at the desk in his home, reviewing the town plans. There was a knock at the door. He didn't pay much attention to it though. He heard his butler answer, the butler was aware Douglas was not to be disturbed at this time, unless of course it was an emergency. Whether or not what happened next falls into the category of an emergency or not is a bit unknown, but the fact of the matter is the Mayor was disturbed none the less. Moments after he heard the butler answer the door he heard a gunshot. Then all was silent. Douglas scrambled over to his closet where he kept his rifle. He checked it to make sure it was loaded, which it was, and went back to his desk where he crouched behind and waited in silence.

The sounds of footsteps were echoing through the hallway, they were moving at a casual pace. As the steps got closer, Douglas began to feel nervous. He had never shot anybody before, but it wasn't that fact that was truly bothering him, it was the fact that he, himself had never been shot before. It was a risk you take when you get involved with politics, but when you really get down to it, it's a risk you take when you get involved with life.

The Mayor's office was the third door down the hallway. It was on the left. The steps made it to the first door when they stopped. Next was the sound of that first door getting kicked in, the sound of the steps returned. They were in the first room.

Douglas could hear some stuff being tossed around, but the noise didn't stay in that room for long.

The steps were leaving the room, they were coming back towards Douglas. The next door was kicked in, it was followed by a similar sound to the last one, just a little bit louder this time. Sweat began to pour down his face, he readied his rifle and aimed for the door. He was ready.

The steps left the second room and began coming towards the third door. The winning door. When the steps got to the outside of the door, they stopped once again. Douglas could see as much as a shadow through the crack at the bottom. There was just less than two seconds of complete silence, which seemed a hell of a lot longer. Douglas had time to think about his entire life in that moment, but every moment comes to an end, and the rest happened fast.

The door burst open and Douglas fired. The intruder was quick to get out of the way. Douglas could hear him doing something, but wasn't sure what it was.

"State your name stranger." Douglas shouted.

"What the hell for?" was his response," it's nothing your gonna remember."

"What makes you so sure about that?"

"You need a brain to remember, and in a few seconds it's gonna be all over that window there behind you."

Douglas began to speak, but just as he opened his mouth the intruder was back in the doorway, gun in hand, firing shots. Douglas ducked down as the window shattered behind him. He popped back up to fire some shots of his own, but it was too late, the intruder had already ducked out of the way.

"You son of a bitch," Douglas shouted as he ducked back behind his desk, "I just had that window cleaned."

"That window should be the least of your concerns, there's Heaven and then there's Hell, be concerned about that."

"Ah, so you're a praying man."

"No, I didn't say that."

"But Heaven and Hell concerns you?"

"I didn't say that either, I said it's your concern."

The intruder popped back out and fired two shots this time, Douglas heard one of them go past his head when it shot through the desk and into the floor. The other bullet missed completely.

The intruder began to ever so slowly enter the room, one cautious step at a time. Douglas stayed behind the desk. He was eyeing the giant hole in the wall, where the window used to be, deciding just how he would make his exit.

"What does my life mean to you?" Asked Douglas

"Don't mean shit"

"Then why are you doing this?"

"It's just something that needs to be done."

Douglas knew he was awfully close now, way too close. He got ready to make a run for the window, but then he decided to make an offer. "I suppose there's no way I could talk my way out of this."

"Nope."

"Money?"

"Nope."

"Why?"

"You don't got enough."

"Perhaps you don't understand the value of my bank account?"

"I don't have to, you're a dead man, dead men don't have bank accounts."

Douglas figured he was history if he didn't make his move right now. He jumped for the window as the intruder fired his last shot. He was a good shot. If things hadn't happened the way they did at the moment it happened, Douglas would have been the dead man the intruder was talking about.

Luckily for the Mayor, moments before that last shot was fired, somebody had been approaching from behind. Just as the trigger was pulled, that body threw itself into the intruder, sending both of them to the ground.

Douglas retreated from the window with haste, grabbing the rifle he left under the desk. He saw a young lady getting off of the ground. The intruder had dropped his gun, he was reaching for it when Douglas came around and plugged him in the face with the other end of his rifle. Two teeth spilled out when his head hit the floor, he wouldn't notice that until later on though, when he woke up at the Elk's Town jail house.

"Holy shit!" Douglas shouted, "Where in the bloody hell did you come from?"

"I was on my way home to change when I heard gunshots coming from your house, there was another man shot dead earlier today."

"Who?"

"Carl"

"Oh my lord," Douglas had to take a seat. He found one on the corner of his desk, "just what the hell's going on here?"

"I'm not too sure."

"You look familiar, I know you."

"Yes you do, I live just two houses up that way." she pointed to the direction of her house.

"Yes, that's right, you took over your Daddy's farm five years back, your nephew Cordell came up to stay with you for a while."

"That's right sir."

"Blake?" asked the Mayor, "that's your name, right?"

"No sir, its Deputy."

4

"What in the hell do you think you're doing!?" Mayor Douglas shouted at Andrew as they stood outside the jailhouse. The intruder was safely tucked away in a cell as Blake watched them argue through the window. "A girl? A fucking girl?"

"With all due respect Mayor Douglas, you need to calm your ass down," Andrew replied, "Do you need to be reminded that the girl saved your life."

"Yes, this is true," Douglas spoke softer now, "but my life is dedicated to this town, my life wouldn't be worth living if this town had a female deputy."

"Well I'm gonna have to disagree with you on that one sir, I think this town would do just damn fine," Andrew lied, but the dedication of the mayor not wanting to have a female deputy made Andrew want to have her more, "maybe it could be like a tourist attraction."

"It's an attraction meant for the circus."

"Listen Doug, now it's like I explained, I never intended for her to be a deputy. Carl was found murdered and I had to deputize the crowd standing around me to bring in the killer. I was speaking to the men when I did it, but she misunderstood that. But regardless of however it became that way, I think she proved herself to be somewhat of a hero."

"Are you suggesting you give her a chance?"

"No sir, she had her chance, I'm suggesting I keep her."

The Mayor wasn't pleased with this decision, but he wasn't unimpressed. "You do what you need to do Marshall, but don't you dare fuck up my town." The mayor pulled out a cigarette and lit it up. He offered one to Andrew, Andrew declined, and with that, the Mayor was on his way.

Andrew watched him leave, thinking about what a terrible habit that tobacco was, and then he thought about the day. He turned back toward the jailhouse and saw Blake watching out the window.

"Well," he thought to himself, "I guess you got some shit to deal with."

Andrew walked back into the building. There was a couple of desks right at the front of the room. One of them was his, that's where he sat down. It was one big open room, with cells running across the back wall. The intruder was stuffed in the middle one, and just to the left was Cattleman. Cattleman made a regular appearance in the Elks Town jailhouse. He wasn't a bad man, he just made bad decisions. Everybody wanted him to succeed, but expected him to fail.

"Well," Andrew spoke to Blake, "what do you figure?"

"I figure I want to protect this town." Blake replied.

"Yeah, I understand that."

They were both quiet for a moment. Andrew looked at her and thought real hard, she looked back with the face of someone who could seriously hold down the law. Andrew reached into a bucket he kept under his desk, when his hand came back out, there was a badge in it. He tossed it across the table where it landed within Blake's reach. Then he asked her, "When can you start?"

5

It wasn't a busy day at the saloon, but it wasn't slow either. It had been an eventful day and people were upset about the loss of their beloved friend Carl, and in Elks Town, the best way to get rid of your sorrows is to drown them.

In the corner Cordell the piano man was playing his song on the piano. He wasn't too much in the mood for playing, and wasn't sure if the people were in the mood for listening, so he finished his song and went to find himself a seat at the bar. Feng the bartender never asked, he just brought him a beer.

"Here pal," Feng said, "this one's on the house."

Cordell thanked him and took a big gulp out of his glass, the type of gulp that would drown a sorrow. It was moments later that Blake walked in. Cordell didn't notice, but every other man in the place did. She made her way across the room to where Cordell sat, many eyes followed.

"How are you doing?" Blake asked.

"Oh, hey Auntie, "Said Cordell as he looked up at her, then his face was crossed with confusion, "wait, what are you doing here?"

"I needed to talk to you."

"About what?" asked Cordell.

"Not in here," said Blake, "let's go outside."

Cordell threw back the remainder of his drink and followed his Auntie out the door. Everybody watched her leave, once she was gone, they all returned to whatever it was they were doing before she broke their concentration.

Outside the saloon Blake began to talk.

"I got a job today Cordell."

"A job?, doing what?"

"I'm the new deputy of Elks Town."

"No shit eh?" said Cordell, Blake didn't approve of his language, so she fixed him with a slap across the face.

"Now you know better than to talk like that." she scolded.

"I'm sorry Auntie, I don't know what I was thinking, I guess my minds just somewhere else right now, you know, with what happened to Carl and all, wait, is it true what the people are saying about you? Did you really save the Mayor?"

"Well I'm the new deputy ain't I?"

"That is so cool," Cordell spoke with little excitement in his voice, he meant to be happier for her, he was proud of his Auntie, it was just a rough day.

"Are you going to be all right?" asked Blake.

"Yeah, yeah, I think I'll be good."

"He was a good man."

"Carl?"

"Yeah."

"I know."

Blake gave Cordell a hug and a kiss on the forehead.

"I'm gonna get going now," said Blake as she began to walk away, "Don't come home too late, I start work early in the morning."

"What if people want to hear the piano?"

"Then I guess you had better start playing," she said as she gave him a smile, "Goodnight Cordell."

"Goodnight Auntie."

Blake walked into the night. Cordell took a moment to look at the sky. He thought and then he walked back into the saloon. A few minutes later the piano began to play as the citizens of Elks town drank away their sorrow, with every drop it took.

6

Meloche sat quietly in his cell. It's what he did ever since he woke up in there. He noticed a couple of his teeth were missing, but it didn't bother him. What was bothering him was the man in the cell next to him. He hadn't stopped talking for a long time, and when he wasn't talking it was replaced with obnoxious singing or banging and clanging. This was really beginning to piss Meloche off. At this moment in particular, Cattleman was trying to strike up a conversation.

"Hey," Cattleman hollered through the bars, "hey bad boy, what are you doing over there?" Meloche thought about ignoring him, but didn't think that would do any good.

"I'm thinking of ways to make you stop talking," Meloche replied, "preferably in ways that would prevent you from talking permanently."

"Oh yeah," said Cattleman, "your a real bad boy eh?"

"The baddest"

"Well what if I tell you that I don't think you're so bad?" Cattleman asked, "what if I tell you I think you're nothing but a little bitch?"

"Then I guess you're going to get your ass kicked by what you believe appears to be a little bitch."

"Speaking of getting ass kicked by a little bitch, tell me how exactly you ended up in here."

Meloche was quiet now, he was pissed off. His ears began to turn red as he tried to control his anger, thinking of ways to kill the man next to him. That was something he prided himself in, when he wanted somebody dead, they would end up dead. A lot of people died from the hands of Meloche, and he had done it in many different ways. Carl was victim Thirty Four, the Mayor was supposed to be thirty five, but the way things were going right now he might have to push him to thirty six.

"What's the matter?" asked Cattleman, "you don't want to talk anymore?"

Meloche made no response, just sat and stared forward as he had before. That ended up being what he did for the majority of his time spent at Elks Town jailhouse.

"Fine, that's all right with me," said Cattleman, "I was getting tired of talking to you anyway."

Cattleman began back into one of his tunes, Meloche couldn't tell you what it was, other than annoying. He had never heard the song before. He couldn't tell the melody he was playing, when he banged on the bars and made odd humming noises. But what he could tell you was that Cattleman was going to die.

7

Andrew and Blake were sitting at his desk in the jailhouse. He was going over some rules and regulations with her when Cordell walked in.

"Good afternoon," greeted Cordell.

"Well how's the town's best piano player doing today?" asked Andrew.

"All is good sir, I hope your training my Auntie well," said Cordell

"I would certainly hope so," Andrew replied, "the whole town depends on it." Andrew turned to Blake, "Listen, I was just about to head over to the saloon to get some lunch, you want me to bring you back something?"

"No," said Blake, "I'll be fine, how long are you going to be?"

"Oh I reckon it won't be much more than an hour," Andrew said. "You two take care."

Andrew put his hat on and headed out the door. Cattleman was sleeping in his cell, while Meloche sat still in his signature position. Cordell walked over and sat at the chair in front of Andrew's desk.

"Well, how are things going for you?" asked Cordell

"It's very well Cordell," Blake said, "How is your day going?"

"It actually just started, but it feels like it's going to be swell."

"I assume you had a late night last night."

"Not too late, but it was late none the less."

"Hey!!" Cattleman shouted from his cell, "do you two want to keep it down; I'm trying to get some shut eye."

"You can shut the fuck up Cattleman," Blake shouted, "if you don't want to be here then maybe you should quit finding your way in."

Just then Tony came stumbling in. "Marshal!" Tony was screaming, "Where's the Marshal?"

"He just stepped out," said Blake, "but I'm sure it's nothing I can't help you with."

"Well, I guess you're going to have to," Tony slurred.

"What's the problem?" asked Blake.

"I got cheated by wild Rob, we was playing poker and he cheated, so I called him on it and he didn't like that very much, so he pulls out his pistol and starts talking about how he's going to shoot the place up."

"Where did this happen?" Blake was growing more concerned, everybody in town was used to Tony's shenanigans, a shenanigan was what she was inclined to play this off as, but then again, with Tony you never could be certain.

"It was at my house."

"Where is he now?"

"He still in my house, waving his pistol around, probably shooting all of my possessions."

"Well all right," said Blake as she got onto her feet and put on her hat, "let's go on down there and see if we can't settle him down." Blake looked over at Cordell, "you mind doing me a favour and wait around here until I get back?"

"I'm not too sure I'm qualified," Cordell said.

"You'll be all right, the bad guys are all locked up and I won't even be long." Blake assured him.

"Well, yeah, okay I guess I could do that, but on one condition."

"And what might that be?"

"I want a gun."

"A gun?"

"Yeah, just in case shit."

Blake reached out and slapped Cordell in the mouth, "What did I tell you about that language of yours?"

"I'm sorry, but can I have one?" Cordell begged.

Blake thought and then a smile came across her face. Cordell smiled back, he knew what that smile meant when he seen it. It was the same smile she gave when he asked for a donkey three years back. Shortly after that smile, he got his donkey, just as shortly after the smile he got just now she reached under the desk and placed a pistol on top of it.

"I'll be good with it, I promise." Cordell said, as he reached to pick it up.

"Oh I know you will, or I might just have to shoot you with it," Blake was joking, Cordell knew, but Tony wasn't sure. "All right Tony, let's get going."

Tony and Blake left the jailhouse, Cordell watched them and began spinning his pistol around his finger like a cowboy. Cattleman was watching this all. A smile came across his face as well.

"AAAAARGGGHH!!!" Cattleman screamed as he dropped himself onto the floor, Cordell turned around and saw Cattleman grabbing at his throat as if he was choking, "help me."

Cordell stuck his pistol in his trousers and walked over to Cattleman's cell.

"What's the matter with you?" Cordell asked.

"I-don't-know," Cattleman said between gasped breaths, "you got.. to get.. me to the doctor," doctor came out the hardest, but when he pronounced it, it sounded more like doctah.

"The doctor?, I can go get him." Cordell said.

"No," said Cattleman, "there isn't enough time; you got to take me to him."

"Well, I don't even know how to get you out."

"The key," Cattleman pointed over towards the left side of the building where the keys were hanging, "it's over there, up on the wall."

Cordell walked over to the wall, as the room was filled with the sound of Cattleman coughing, and took hold of the key. He slowly walked back towards Cattleman's cell, but was unsure of himself.

"I'm not sure if I should be doing this." Cordell said.

"You gotta, I'm dying!!" Cattleman cried, "You just can't leave me here to die."

Cordell stood in front of Cattleman's cell with the key in his hand, He started to place it into the key hole when he came to a halt. Cattleman watched in awe.

"What the hell did you stop for?"

"Why'd you stop coughing?"

"I didn't," Cattleman cried as he started coughing again, as if he could still pull this trick off.

"Fuck you Cattleman," Cordell said as he took the key away from the lock and began his journey across the room to put it back.

"No. fuck you pussy," Cattleman yelled back, he was about to settle back down onto his bench, but didn't get a chance. Cordell was only a few steps away when Meloche grabbed him through the bars and held him tight with his arm wrapped all the way around his throat. Cordell tried to grab his pistol, but it was already in Meloche's other hand pressed tight to his temple.

"Open the cage," Meloche demanded.

"I can't," Cordell replied.

Meloche brought the gun down, aimed it at the back of Cordell's knee, and squeezed the trigger. Blood and bits of his knee cap scattered across the floor as the room filled with a scream from Cordell.

"Open the cage," Meloche repeated with the same emotionless tone. Cordell continued screaming as he fumbled with the key, trying to get it into the lock. This didn't bother Meloche, as long as it was getting done, it didn't bother him at all. Patience was on his side. Eventually Cordell got the key in and unlocked the door. Meloche immediately released Cordell and let him drop to the ground, he held his leg and screamed some more in agonizing pain. Meloche stepped out of his cell and adjusted his attire. He then turned to look at Cattleman who was watching it all, in complete shock. Meloche raised the pistol and shot Cattleman in his big toe. Cattleman took hold of his foot and began some screams of his own. Meloche watched him for a moment, he waited for Cattleman to settle down, gain his composure a bit, and when this happened he got a chance to look Meloche in the eye. At this point Cattleman learned that Meloche was never meant to be fucked with, a lesson learned too late. Meloche still had the pistol pointed at him. He squeezed the trigger again; there were no screams this time. He turned his attention back to Cordell, and that was when the piano player died.

8

Andrew was finishing his burger at the saloon at approximately the same time Meloche took his final shot, ending Cordell. It was a tasty burger. He put his hat on and made his way back to the jailhouse. He wasn't ready for what he saw. He didn't see Blake's body in the mess, which was good, but she wasn't there at all, and that was bad.

Something terrible had happened here, and a very dangerous man was on the loose. Andrew had a very good feeling of where he was going, if he wasn't already there. He quickly got onto his horse and was off to the Mayor's house, praying that he wasn't too late.

9

Mayor Douglas was in the back yard tending his garden when the figure of a man appeared behind him, performing a casual walk, with a pick axe in hand. Douglas was into deep thought while he tended his garden, completely oblivious to what was going on behind him. If he would of looked up at any point in time between the three minutes it took for Meloche to walk up there, he might of lived a few years longer, but that was only a what if, and it wasn't.

If Douglas would of stayed perfectly still when Meloche brought the pick axe down over his head, it would of been the best case scenario for the Mayors current situation, but it just so happened that he took notice to the shadow above him, moments before the pick axe came down with intentions of crushing through his skull and striking his brain. But Douglas had turned, altering the point of impact from his head to the inner part of his shoulder. The pick axe went all the way through; it was now sticking through his shoulder and out his armpit. Douglas screamed. Meloche put his foot on the Mayors face and yanked out his weapon, tearing open Douglas even more. There was a huge gash in his shoulder, almost a separation between his arm and the rest of his body. All he could do was lay there, he couldn't even scream anymore. He was still very much alive; he was just going into shock.

As he lay there, Meloche came at him again. This time digging into his stomach. Douglas felt it, but at this point in time, he didn't give a shit. There was no recovering from this, he was a cooked turkey. Meloche set down the axe and began digging through the Mayors pockets. Douglas just watched. When Meloche found what he was looking for, his hand came out with a package of cigarettes. He took one out and placed it into his mouth, he took out another one and offered it to the Mayor. He got no response, so he just placed it in his lips. It hung there for a moment, then it just fell off. Meloche lit the cigarette he had for himself and took a seat beside the dying man.

"I just want you to know something," Meloche said, "I want you to know I got nothing against you, this was just business, that's all, nothing else. I don't reckon that means a thing to you, not at this point anyway.," Meloche took another puff of his cigarette, "I did enjoy it though. My little stay here at Elks town, it's a nice place you got here," Meloche smiled, then he looked down into the Mayors eyes, but there was nothing there anymore. Meloche wondered how long he had been talking, before Douglas made his way to the other side. He put out his cigarette and got to his feet. He wondered if Douglas really was dead, or just pretending, there was a very low risk that he could make it. Slim chances, but a chance is still a chance.

The sound of a galloping horse was heading towards him quite quickly. There was no hesitation. Meloche lifted the pick axe and brought it down through the Mayors left eye. It went all the way through and pinned him to the ground.

By the time Andrew had got to the house, Meloche had completed his last visit to Elks town.

10

40 Years Later

"And that was the last I heard of him." Andrew put out his cigarette. Wendy sat across the table with a speechless look stuck in her face, the face matched her comments. There was more than a tiny bit of silence for the next few moments, and then she came to.

"Wait," she asked, "that's it?"

"Yeah, that would be the general gist of things," Andrew had another cigarette in his hand, he was playing with it as he spoke, "that's what you wanted to know, right? I had been put under the impression that you're trying to put a book together about this Meloche guy. Gathering his stories and what not, that's why your here, right?"

"Well, yes, in that sense it's the general gist of things, but you left too many things open, like Blake, what happened with her?"

"I got my reason for leaving that out, other than the fact that she's not who you came to hear about, I think there was enough killing in my story, don't feel much like talking about death anymore.

"You can't just leave it like that, I gotta know." Wendy said. Andrew looked at her with a bit of disgust, but mostly understanding.

"She had come back to the jailhouse after I had left for the Mayor's house. She saw Cordell, she saw what happened to him. She couldn't handle it, went a little crazy. Cordell was all she had, without him there was nobody but her and the farm.

She blamed herself for what happened, by leaving him in charge when she knew damn well that was a bad idea. She started keeping to herself a lot, just shut herself up in that little house. People would go visit, but she wouldn't accept any company. At this point she got fairly heavy into the booze. It got to the point where the only time you could see her was when she was on her way to the saloon to bring home some whiskey. Soon after that she wasn't coming out at all. I'd say all that happened within a month's time. After nobody had seen or heard from her in a week somebody decided to go to her house and check on her, but she already checked out. I found her hanging from the ceiling," Andrew thought for a moment, "You know, I just heard some folks are building a new house on the land where that house stood before the disaster." "Wait, you found her?"

"I was the Marshal." Both of them sat in silence for a moment. Andrew was tired of talking, and Wendy was just letting it all sink in.

"That's a sad story." Wendy said when she finally spoke.

"It's the story you asked for."

"Anything more about Meloche?"

"Well he continued on with his ways as far as I know. He was good at what he did though, never got caught, at least it's not in any records. I used to look up on that from time to time. Back when I was concerned about things. His Elk town days were certainly over. You know, every now and again I would hear some stories about these grisly murders, there was no witnesses to these events, but deep down in my soul, I knew it was him."

"Do you think he's still around today?"

"I wouldn't think so, I would assume father time took him by now, but then again, here I am. I guess he could be, but if he is I would assume him to be too old to be doing what he was put on this earth to do. I haven't heard anything evil enough that would bring any type of acknowledgement to his existence. But I think he's gone now. There's not many left from my era, or even the generation beneath me. I'm not too sure why I'm still living, ninety years is just too long, too long on this planet, at least this here part of it."

"And the death of the Mayor, that was the reason for the downfall of Elks town?"

"No, that's just what started it."

"Why are people coming back?"

"I can think of a number of reasons. Maybe because of the new name, they feel comfortable considering it as a different place. Maybe it represents second chances, a lot of people depend on that second chance in life, but I think it's the land. There's something I don't understand about the land. It's almost alive and has the ability to lure people in. Maybe it's just the land calling them back. Because evil is real. It exists, and it needs a home."

"You retired at sixty three?"

"That's correct."

"So what have you done since then?"

"Well, I guess I've done the same thing I've been doing my entire life."

"And what is that?"

"I'm waiting to die." Andrew said, as he lit another cigarette.

TO CATCH
A DREAM

1

Jake Livingston sat in his bed with one eye closed, and his favourite book in front of him. He knew the story well, so well in fact, he never had to read the words anymore. Just looked at the pictures, and made up a story.

The actual story was about a train that had no friends. It had to go on adventures all by its lonesome. Jake found this story so interesting because it was something he could relate to. He could read of course, as a matter of fact at seven years old he was the finest reader out of all his second grade class, it was just that he got bored with repetitiveness and found it to be more entertaining with new adventures. Reading wasn't all he was good at, there was science, history and math as well. He dazzled all of it, well… almost all of it. There was one thing he was a complete failure to, one thing that was his constant downfall, one thing that ruined it all, and that one thing was physical education… gym class. He always tried, he tried harder than "The Little Engine that could," but he couldn't. The worst part of it was, there was no seriousness to gym class, it was all fun and games. He was just too weak, a last one picked for the team type of situation. Jake did have asthma though, a bad case of it, but even if this asthma didn't exist, his skills would remain the same. So book smart was his gig.

Jake didn't have any friends, his father left before he was born and his mother never spoke to her family. From what he understood through gossip and loose lips, was that when she got pregnant with him, her family sort of disowned her, simply based on the fact that she wasn't wedded. She went her own way after that, and took Jake with her. So he was all she had, she was all he had, and that's all they needed. There was however, someone else who played a crucial role in Jake's life. Not the friend, not the lover, but the bully. Joe Luthor.

Joe was in Jake's class, Joe was a year older than everybody else in class. Because of this, Joe felt he could demand a special kind of respect, based on him being somewhat of an elder to his peers. Should have been the other way around though. Joe was there because he had failed the last time around, he failed all of it, well almost all of it. There was gym class.

People always have this temporary goal, this want of something at a certain time on their life, it becomes their ultimate goal. Sometimes the things people want, are the things they can't have. When they can't have these things, they get certain feelings towards the people who can and do. They realize there is just no way of acquiring such things. Jealousy runs its course.

Joe's goal was to be smart, he wanted to be brilliant, but he wasn't and never would be. Many reasons exist for this to be his situation. A majority of it comes from inside his home, it was his lifestyle. It wasn't his fault, that's just the way it was, making Joe the way he was, which didn't make him a very nice fellow.

Jake had these smarts that Joe so long destined for. Jake's I.Q. made Joe incredibly jealous, but Joe's I.Q was so low, that he didn't even know he was jealous, all he knew was that he didn't like him, so he didn't like him. Joe's lifestyle taught him to deal with situations in one form, that form was physical, very physical. You had to be tough to live at Joe's house, there was no other choice.

That's why as Jake sat on his bed and looked at his book that fine evening, he was looking with one eye. The other one had swollen shut on him, turned a nasty colour too. Jake was under the impression that his mother was under the impression that he had run into some playground equipment at recess. That was the story he told, a story told out of fear. Fear of Joe and his retaliation. That's what Joe called it. Most likely because it was one of the few big words Joe knew, so he used it as much as possible. If he couldn't be smart, he could at least sound smart. Joe had retaliation for everything. If you didn't give Joe what he wanted when he asked, there was retaliation for that, when you didn't take the fall for something he did, there was retaliation for that, and when you told on him for giving you a black eye, you better believe there's retaliation for that.

Regardless of the reason he told the lie to his mother, she still knew the truth, not the full truth, as in she didn't know who had done this to him, she just knew there was no truth to Jake's story.

She wondered why he would lie, thought long and hard about what was going on. After careful thought and consideration, she decided that leaving this to Jake was the right decision. She did it based on the facts that he was trying to keep it from her. Jake was a good kid. She didn't understand why he would lie without a good reason. If it happened again, she would most likely feel obligated to change her decision. But they're just kids, how bad could it get? So she allowed Jake to tell his story the way it was, and leave him to fight his own battle.

This wasn't the only problem in Jake's life, as you probably know, all things, good or bad, always come in three's. Jake's next big issue which leads to the real reason he was up so late with his book. Looking at the pictures. His favourite pictures. The pictures of nice things, like cotton candy, puppy dogs and rainbows, was because Jake suffered from a serious case of night terrors. That problem had been going on for quite some time.

At certain points in the seasons it would calm down a bit and he would have some peaceful sleeps, but in reality those were just the dreams he couldn't remember. As far back as time went, Jake had nightmares every single night of his entire life. But fortunately for Jake, that was all about to change.

Jake heard his mother coming up the stairs, he supposed she was coming to tuck him in, he supposed she was going to make him put away his book and make him go to sleep, he supposed the night terrors would begin. He was right about two of those things.

"Hey buddy" Jake looked up and saw his mother standing by the door.

"Hi mom," Jake replied, "what are the chances of me staying up a little bit longer?"

"About as good as us winning the lottery I suppose," she responded. This made Jake smile which warmed her heart. She walked further into the room, this is when Jake noticed she was carrying a box, it was a shoe box. Jake's curiosity grew as she sat down beside him on the bed.

"What's in the box?" Jake asked.

"Well, the people I work with know about how you've been having troubles sleeping," this upset Jake a bit, he didn't like when his mother would talk to people about his personal life, but he didn't show it, not this time, "do you remember Mrs. Cardinal, from the Christmas party?"

Jake thought back to the Christmas party her work had put on, all of the children of the parents got to go to the bowling alley for the afternoon following a brunch with Santa Claus. He remembered the Aboriginal lady who was helping Santa hand out presents, his mother had introduced him to her as Mrs. Cardinal.

"Yes, I remember" Jake replied.

"Well, she made this for you." Jake's mother opened the box and pulled out a beautiful piece of art. It was a large brass circle wrapped in blue thread. There was a smaller brass circle in the middle and dark blue threads extended from the larger circle to the middle circle with a hypnotizing pattern, it kind of reminded him of a spider web, only this was more pleasant to look at. Beads bordered the edge of the large circle with a mixture of a darker blue and baby blue. Threads hung down from the bottom with a few more beads and feathers.

"Do you like it?" his mom asked.

"Yeah, but what is it?"

"This, my son, is a dream catcher, "she replied," you see, what it does is hang on the wall above your bed so when you go to sleep all of the bad dreams get caught in the webbing, and only the good ones can come through"

"Does it work?" Jake asked "well, there's only one way to find out."

Jake smiled. He wasn't sure if it would work or not, but after the years of terrible sleeps, he was definitely willing to give it a try, he couldn't see how it would make things worse.

"Can you hang it up right now?" Jake asked.

"Absolutely," His mother said, she had already planned on doing this and earlier while Jake was playing outside she had pounded a nail in the wall above his bed. She reached over her son and hung it up. Jake was pleased.

"Goodnight son," she said as she kissed him on the cheek.

"Goodnight mom," Jake said back and for the first time comfortably laid down to welcome sleep.

He felt it was working already or maybe it was just wishful thinking, but by the time Jake's mother had reached the door to leave the room and shut the light, Jake was already in la la land.

"Sweet dreams," she whispered as she shut off the light. That night Jake slept like a baby.

2

When Jake woke up, he wasn't too sure what was going on. It was as if he had just closed his eyes and opened them. But it was different now, it wasn't dark anymore. The sun was just beginning to rise as it spilled the days first light through the window. This puzzled Jake for a moment, but as he awoke things slowly fell into place. Jake looked up at the dreamcatcher. The strings hanging down seemed to be a bit tangled. Jake took the time to straighten them out and smiled. He was under the impression that it was going to be a good day. He was wrong about that.

Jake left his room and headed down the hall, He could smell bacon coming from the kitchen. This was another level of excitement for Jake. Usually it was cereal for breakfast, but today he was getting a hot meal. What excited him even more was every time his mother cooked bacon, she would make pancakes as well, and pancakes were his favourite. When he got halfway through the hall, he couldn't contain himself any longer and made a mad dash for the kitchen. Once he got there, he was the happiest he would be all day.

"Good morning sunshine," said his mother as she turned around from the stove

"Good morning mom," Jake said as he sat down at the table, "it sounded like you slept well last night."

"I did, I think so," Jake responded.

"Why do you only think so," she asked.

"I don't remember anything, it was as if I didn't dream at all."

"So is it safe to say it worked?"

"It's safe to say so," Jake said as his smile that couldn't get any bigger, got bigger.

"Great," his mother said with a similar smile, as she brought over a plate of eggs, bacon and pancakes. She set it in front of her son. Jake reached for the syrup. It had already been waiting for him at the table. Moments later the pancakes began to drown in the great flood of syrup, courtesy of Jake. It was times like this when Jake would forget what it meant to be a gentleman and began to devour his meal. By the time his mother had returned to the table with a tall glass of orange juice for him, which took no time at all, half of his breakfast was already gone.

"Thank you mom," managed to slip out of Jake's lips somewhere between filling his face and taking a breath. Children aren't meant to be gentlemen, his mother thought as she smiled, watching her child eat like a lunatic. These were the moments that made life worth living, the cherished memories. There's no better way to start your day than with laughter and smiles, and if that's what made him smile, then that's what made her laugh. It was a very happy morning.

After breakfast he went upstairs to get dressed for school. He got all of his clothes on, put all of his books in his back pack. He was about to leave the room when the dreamcatcher caught his attention. It was still hanging peacefully in the exact same place his mother had placed it. But the strings at the bottom were all tangled up again. Jake looked over to his window to see if perhaps a draft had come through and done this, but the window was closed. Jake walked over to it for a closer examination.

"Jake!!!, you're going to miss the bus," his mother hollered from the kitchen. Jake untangled the strings and ran out of the room, down the hall and out the door, but not before taking the time to kiss his mother good bye. His mother had to get to work as well, so moments after Jake's departure she made her routine inspections to make sure the windows were closed, the lights were off, and nothing was left on. Exactly seven minutes after Jake had left his room, Jakes mother poked her head in and wondered why the threads hanging down from the dreamcatcher were in tangles. She only wondered for a moment though, she had a job to get to and she was running late.

When Jake got to the bus stop, which was located at mailbox just down the road, Susie and Jasmine were there playing a game with a string called cat's cradle. Jake never understood that game, but he never understood Susie and Jasmine either, so he just let it be.

"Good Morning Jake," they both said oddly at the same time.

"Good Morning," Jake replied with not much enthusiasm.

"Are you gonna get beat up again today?" Susie asked as Jasmine snickered. Jake didn't reply to this. There were no further comments after that. He heard them whispering to each other, whether or not they were talking about him wasn't any of his concern. It wasn't long after that till the bus was spotted coming around the corner. It pulled up to the stop and swung its doors open. Susie and Jasmine slowly climbed the steps. Jake was just about to climb aboard when he heard someone yelling in the distance. Well it wasn't just someone, Jake knew exactly who it was, little Timmy. It wasn't good for Timmy to run as he had a bad case of asthma as well.

"Wait for me!!!!" Timmy hollered as he ran as fast as he could, which wasn't fast at all.

"Slow down," Jake yelled, "do you want to get an asthma attack?" Timmy must have taken this into consideration because he slowed down to a light jog after that. Jake climbed aboard and told Harold the bus driver that Timmy was still coming. Harold mumbled something, Jake couldn't quite make it out under the stale stench of whiskey that was in his breath. Jake found his seat halfway to the back of the bus and sat down. He could still hear Jasmine and Susie snickering but it sounded like Timmy was the victim of their conversation this time. For some reason that made Jake more upset than when they were teasing about him. Timmy climbed aboard and apologized for being late, he was giving Harold an excuse which Harold didn't seem to care about as he closed the door, put the bus into gear, and was on his way. Timmy never got a chance to sit down, he was sent stumbling down the aisle where he almost fell, he would of fell had there not been any seats to catch himself on. A few of the children snickered. Timmy felt a little embarrassed. He quickly regained his balance, trotted down the aisle, and found his seat.

The rest of the ride was fairly quiet. The odd laughter every now and then from the other children telling knock knock jokes or speaking of the events that took place from the time they got off the bus yesterday, until the time they got back on. Some kids were struggling to complete assignments that were due that day and other kids, such as Jake, sat in silence. They all had their own things to do and think about. Jake's thoughts were rested on what happens when the bus reaches the school yard and he gets off. There were lots of children that attended the school and teachers weren't always around. Jake was in fear, not the kind of fear his dreams held, but a fear in reality. You can't wake up from reality, and in that reality was a kid called Joe.

Joe's home life was far from great, he had a father who was constantly in and out of the prison system, and when he was out he wasn't around. He was too busy trying to find another way in. His mother was a free bird, but came around just a little bit more than his father did, and most her time there was spent in her bedroom with the door closed. He didn't like it, but he didn't mind it either. Whenever she was around there was alcohol and drugs.

He didn't know what kind, he just knew it was white and she sucked it all in her nose. There were a few times when Joe thought she had died. One of those times was when he woke up to find her laying on the living room floor, nestled in a pile of her own vomit. It smelt bad, Joe didn't know what to do, so he turned on the television. He sat for a few hours like that. Eventually she woke up, neither one of them said a word. She just got up, went to her room and closed the door.

When there were no drugs or alcohol, it was replaced with yelling and screaming. He could expect a beating too. Not necessarily a beating, she would just do something outrageous. She had little bursts of crazy, it was scary.

There was the time Joe was in the kitchen eating cereal, he heard her door open, she came running out into the kitchen and slapped Joe's face hard enough for him to fall out of his chair. She watched him on the floor, Joe didn't even cry, he just stared back at her. It looked like she was going to do something else, but then she didn't. She just walked on back to her room and closed the door.

Later he would find out she had done that because of his father, she was just angry at him and they looked close enough alike that she decided to just up and pop him one. She told him this, she explained to him why she did it and that was all. There was no apology, just an explanation.

Joe didn't ask for an apology, he didn't ask for anything. He knew questions were not allowed. If Joe asked a question, that would make him liable for an attack of some sort. He once asked her when she would be coming back home while she was on her way out, he was answered with a skateboard thrown at him, smacked him pretty good too. Told him to "mind his damn business and just worry about putting his damn skateboard away." Then she slammed the door. Left Joe there crying all alone, blood trickling down his face. He wasn't crying about her hitting him though, he had grown used to that. What Joe was crying about was confusion. His mind couldn't handle what was going on, frustration got the best of him. When his mother picked up the skateboard to throw it, she grabbed it from the spot behind the door, where he was told to store it. It had nothing to do with his skateboard other than the fact that it became a weapon during this encounter. It was retaliation for the asking of the question.

She had retaliation for everything. If he asked her to stop with the booze and drugs, there was retaliation for that. If he woke her up when she was sleeping, there was retaliation for that, and if he asked any questions about anything that was going on in that house, you better believe there was retaliation for that.

Joe didn't understand it all, all he understood was that life was shit. Not for everybody, but for him, so he thought it was only fair to make life shit for someone else. An easy target, someone he could get things out of, like homework and lunch money, and that someone happened to be Jake.

Jake didn't know anything about Joe's home life. Never bothered to ask, never bothered to care. Just gave him what he wanted and hoped he would leave him alone, but it didn't always work like that. Sometimes Jake would hand over every single thing Joe demanded, and if Joe was having a particular bad day, he would feel the need to vent. Rather than talking, Joe found it better to vent with violence. This was the reasoning for yesterdays attack. Joe was just having a bad day and needed a punching bag. Jake worked out well for that.

Twenty three minutes after Timmy stumbled into his seat, the bus pulled up to the school. The doors swung open and out came the children. Most of them laughing and smiling. A few of the older ones looked more grumpy, they were the ones who had grown accustomed to hating school, going on to hating their jobs and eventually hating life. Jake got off and walked as quickly as he could to get inside. He wasn't interested in being seen. Not through anybody's eyes, but Joe's in particular. Jake would be fine though. Joe wouldn't be there yet, Joe wasn't the type to show up on time. Jake already figured this out, but he also figured out that once in a blue moon, things could go a little bit different.

It wasn't until lunchtime when Jake had to face the music of the intolerable bad boy and this day the music wasn't only bad, but it was loud as well. Jake had just gotten to his seat in the cafeteria. He brought his own lunch today in a brown paper bag. He set it on the table and sat down. That's when he heard the voice behind him.

"Heeeeey Jakey." It was Joe, but Jake didn't need to turn around to know that. However, Jake did turn around, just because he knew things would only get worse if he chose to ignore him, "hows your eye?" Joe asked as he approached.

"My eyes fine," Jake replied in a very monotone voice.

"Well that's great news, isn't it?"

"Yeah, it is," Jake said. Joe walked around to the other side of the table Jake was seated at and took a seat himself. He reached across the table and snatched Jakes lunch bag out of his hand before he even had a chance to open it.

"What do we got for lunch today?" Joe asked as he began rifling through the bag, First he pulled out a sandwich.

"What's this?" Joe asked.

"It's a sandwich," Jake replied.

"Well I know that dipshit, I wanna know what kind of sandwich it is."

"Tuna."

"Tuna!!! I hate tuna," Joe cried, as he tossed the sandwich over his shoulder. Next he pulled out an apple, "this is dumb too," Joe tossed the apple in the same direction as the sandwich. Jake watched it land on the floor, it was immediately spotted by some other children who thought it would have been fun to use it for some soccer practice. The sandwich was kicked, squished and stepped on, eventually making its way to the trash. Almost as if it never even had any intentions at all to make it into Jake's stomach.

As the sandwich met its untimely demise, Joe continued to loot Jake's lunch. The next thing Joe's hand pulled out was an apple.

"This is dumb too," Joe tossed the apple in the opposite direction of the sandwich. The apple remained unnoticed as it bounced of some shoes and found itself a nice little corner, between a counter and a wall to tuck itself into. It remained there for quite some time.

Joe continued his search and Jake watched the same results as he tossed away his carrots and celery. Joe peeked into the almost empty bag and was hit with a smile.

"There," Joe said, "now we're talking" Joe pulled out a bag of three cookies, He tore them open and shoved the first one in his mouth. "Oh, this is good," Joe said through a mouthful of mashed cookies. He did the same thing for the other two as Jake sat and watched in silence. "What's the matter Jake?" Joe asked with little concern on his face, "oh, where are my manners, did you want any of that?" Jake didn't reply, he just watched. "Well, it's too late now I guess, I'm sorry buddy," Joe said with zero sincerity, "now, where's the milk?"

"I got no milk," Jake said.

"What do you mean you got no milk?" Joe looked surprised, "what kind of mother packs a kid's lunch without any milk? Especially if it has cookies in it, you do have a mother right?"

"Of course I have a mother, she's an excellent mother," Jake replied. For some reason this offended Joe, it threw him off guard. This resulted in a brief moment of silence, but only brief, and in the moment, any friendly characteristics that Joe had during their lunch date, ceased to exist. Joe leaned across the table to get closer to Jake, and spoke a little softer.

"You listen Jake, I didn't come here to eat lunch with you, to tell you the truth I can't stand you, you think you're some hot shit eh? So much better than everybody else," Joe paused, "well let me tell you something, you're not, you're no better than any other dipshit you see in this room, or any other room you choose to enter in your pathetic life. Now let's get to business. A lot of people are telling me you went to the principal about our little situation yesterday, which I might add, was completely your own fault, and I have witnesses who are more than willing to speak up on my behalf. I also heard you went crying to your mother about it," Joe waited for Jake to speak a defense, but was met with silence, "well don't you got anything to say?"

"I didn't tell anybody, told my mom I ran into some playground equipment," Jake said.

"Oh yeah? Which piece of equipment?"

"I didn't say."

"Why not?"

"She didn't ask."

Joe took a moment to think about the story Jake had told him. It was believable, and Jake wasn't known to tell a lie. He also took into consideration the fact that nobody had told him anything about Jake going to the principal or his mother.

"I sure hope you're not lying to me," Joe said, "cause if you are, you know things are only gonna get worse, you know that, right?"

"Yes Joe," Jake said

"Good," Joe said, "now I don't got all day to sit around and talk to people I don't like to talk to, but I do have a math assignment due tomorrow that you're going to take care of, you know, to smooth things over between us, am I understood?"

"Yeah," Jake said

"Good," Joe got up and pulled a folded piece of paper out of his pocket. He threw it onto the table in front of Jake and started to walk away. Jake watched him and when he was gone, Jake began to break down, not all the way, not even close, but it started. He pulled himself together before any tears had a chance to make an entrance, or before anybody noticed. He didn't have to worry though, nobody noticed. Not even when the sandwich became a toy for the children, they never wondered where it came from, they just knew it was there. In the cafeteria, full of his peers, who were always watching, and always talking, never noticed a thing.

Jake unfolded the paper Joe left for him. It was fifteen multiplication questions. It was the same assignment Jake had already finished. It was an easy one, so easy that it would have been less of a hassle for Jake to just answer the questions then and there, rather than locate his own assignment and copy the answers. Either way, it wasn't a problem. Jake pulled out his pencil when he was struck with a thought. He stopped what he was doing, and just held onto his pencil for a moment. Jake thought, then he wondered, he wondered what would happen if he got the questions wrong. He thought it would be funny to see the look on Joe's face when the teacher presented him with a big ol'goose egg. Then he thought about the consequences, he thought about the retaliation. Jake decided to answer correct, but now wasn't the time. Something wasn't right, something was happening.

Jake put his pencil back into his pocket, cleaned up the garbage from what was left of his so-called lunch. He folded up Joe's homework, put that with his pencil and left the room. All the other children continued to laugh and tell their jokes and stories. Jake went into the washroom and found a stall. He walked in, locked the door, sat on the toilet and broke down after all. He cried until the end of lunch break.

At approximately 3:45 that afternoon Harold pulled his bus up to the same mail box Jake and the children waited at that morning. He drove better in the afternoon because the hangover wasn't as intense anymore, he was also in a better mood. Jake got off along with the other children, without making any conversation. Jasmine and Susie were still being their regular selves, chanting their little girl rhymes making fun of the children who weren't around to defend themselves, along with the ones who were. If Jake knew what a whore was he would have assumed that's what they would grow up to become.

Jake walked into the back door of the eighteenth house which leads into the kitchen. He dropped his bag on the ground and went to the fridge to find a snack. When he opened the fridge door the first thing he laid his eyes upon was the milk.

"What kind of mother sends a boy to school with cookies and No milk?" these words echoed in his head with the voice from a boy he didn't want to hear ever again. Jake closed the fridge. He wasn't hungry anymore.

"Jake?," His mother was shouting from the bedroom, "is that you?"

"Yeah mom."

"How was school?" she asked.

"It was good," Jake lied.

"There's some cookies in the cupboard, I bought the double stuffed kind, your favourite," she seemed quite pleased with herself on providing Jake with something he enjoyed so much. Jake sensed this in her voice and didn't want to upset her so he lied some more.

"I already got to them. Thanks mom."

"You're welcome Hun," she replied.

Jake went to the cupboard and found the cookies, He opened the bag, took out three and buried them in the garbage. Then he grabbed his bag from beside the door, went up the stairs, and into his room. He closed the door and seated himself at his desk.

As he passed by his bed he glanced at his dreamcatcher. He had forgotten about it up until now. How happy it had made him. He was sure he had untangled the threads that morning, but with all the day had taken him through he couldn't quite remember. By the time he thought of untangling them he was already seated at his desk with his books open. First he would complete all of his assignments, then of course he would take care of Joe's.

When all of that was complete he read his book until his mother called him for supper. He lied about how well his day was, told the truth about how good he was doing in his classes and then lied about how he was feeling. He felt good in thinking his mother was under the impression that he was doing so well all around, but his mother knew better than to believe what she was hearing. Other than the grades of course, which proved themselves with the report cards and tests he brought home for her to post on the refrigerator.

After supper was done Jake went outside to play with his toys. When he got bored with that he came inside and watched the television with his mom. She was watching a show about teenagers who were hooked on drugs, but when she heard Jake come in she changed it to the discovery channel. She knew that was his favourite and there just happened to be a special on about sea otters. It was a rather fascinating episode. When the time came for him to brush his teeth, take a bath and get his pajamas on, he did just that.

At first he got quite upset about it being so close to bedtime, but then he remembered the safety of his dreamcatcher and felt rather welcome. So Jake climbed into bed with his favourite book. He looked up at his dreamcatcher partly to admire its beauty and partly to be sure it was there to protect him. He untangled the threads, plopped down and opened his book.

Fifteen minutes had passed before his mother had come to tuck him in, but when she arrived he was already fast asleep. She walked over to the bed and carefully removed his book from his fingers. He stirred a little bit, but remained perfect in his slumber.

"I love you," she whispered to him in his ear. She leaned down and kissed his forehead, Jake smiled, and she smiled too. She watched him for a moment, it was a proud moment for her. Then she got up and left the room shutting off the light on her way out, but not before untangling the threads of the dreamcatcher.

And that's the way things went for a while with Jake. The soon to be whores would play their childish games, little Timmy would struggle to make it to the bus, Jake would get his great marks, and Joe would be Joe.

3

It was about a month later when the cycle broke. The day in particular started the same, and the situations that carried out all followed the same manner. Jake had been doing great on his assignments and of course Joe's as well, in return Joe hadn't laid a finger on Jake. It almost got to a point where Jake was under the impression that Joe was in fact a friend of his. He was after all the only other child anyone would ever see him talking too, and surprisingly they did have something in common, which was neither one of them had any friends. That was the reality that hit Jake on this day in particular. So the whole day carried out and lead up to Jake in his bedroom, with his homework and his cookies.

For some reason, not even known to Jake, he had decided enough was enough. He was tired of the extra homework and he was tired of being scared. He remembered being scared of his dreams, and he remembered how that had come to an end. He thought it never would have, but it did, and it was glorious. With the thought of something that troubles one so deeply being completely eliminated was a tremendous feeling.

As Jake looked up from completing his homework, he caught a glimpse of his dreamcatcher and saw a symbol. A symbol of change, a symbol of peace, a symbol of hope. His night terrors had been in his life a lot longer than Joe had. There was a time before Joe, not long ago, he remembered that. But before the dreamcatcher, he didn't know a time before night terrors. So what this meant to him was that there is a possibility of change.

Jake thought about this for quite some time, as a matter of fact he thought about it for the rest of that evening. He thought about it when he was in bed with his favourite book, while he untangled the threads in his dreamcatcher, while he brushed his teeth, while he watched the television, while he ate his supper, and while he filled out all of the wrong answers on Joe's homework. And then he thought, "What's the worst that could happen?" He thought, but he didn't know.

Two days later Jake was sitting in the cafeteria eating his lunch. He wasn't waiting for Joe, but he was used to his presence around this time. He saw him in the class earlier, but he was real quiet, maybe he was sick or something. When Joe failed to show up for lunch, Jake paid it no mind, he wasn't bothered, not one bit.

So Jake ate his lunch in complete peace. He ate it all, without any fat fingers digging in to any part of his meal and it was glorious. He got so focused into his peaceful meal, that he didn't notice the eyes that were on him the entire time. The same eyes that seen a father through a glass window whenever he got the chance to see him, the same eyes that seen a mother with bruises, different guys every night, and the white stuff left on the coffee table, the same eyes that saw a zero on his homework that morning. The eyes of rage. And those eyes, along with that rage followed Jake all the way to the boy's washroom, and it just so happened that Jake was alone. Someone could have come in at any time, someone could have stopped it. Someone could of, but as fate hands out its cards of luck, it hands out its cards of shit just as well, and on this day, Jake was in the room meant for the card fate had in store for him.

Jake was standing at the urinal doing his business. He heard the door open but paid it no mind. After all it was just the boy's washroom, why would he pay any sort of mind to people coming out and in, especially during lunch hour, that's what it was there for. He finished his business and zipped up. It was this moment that marked the end of anything that could have had potential to make this a good day. Jake turned around to go wash his hands, when he bumped into Joe who had snuck up behind him. Jake looked at him for a moment as nothing happened. This moment seemed like a long time to Jake, as Joe just stared at him. Not only could he see that Joe was pissed off, but he could sense it too. This was the last thing Jake remembered, which I suppose is a good thing, no one would want or should have to go through the events that took place next, but whether or not it was a would of could of should of situation, it happened none the less.

Jake opened his mouth to say something, but due to his lack of memory and Joe's decision making, those words will never be known. Joe's fist came up and cracked Jake in the jaw sending him back into the urinal he had just came from. Jake brought his hands up to his face for protection, but it didn't do any good. Joe grabbed Jakes right arm and twisted it out of the way causing his first broken bone. The pain was tremendous. He didn't move much after that, other than the direction in which Joe would throw him.

Joe delivered a few more punches to Jakes face. There wasn't much left for Jake to do. He was still conscience but incredibly weak. Jake laid on the floor, didn't even bother to get up, which wouldn't have done any good anyway. Joe stood atop of him looking down. Usually the rage would leave him by now, but this time it didn't. Jake had humiliated him with the stupid answers he put on his work. Joe had basted in a world of shame, as the teacher criticized his stupidity. From that moment on all he wanted to do was what he was doing now. What made it scary was he didn't care whether or not he got away with it, and by the looks of things it seemed he was going to get away just fine. But that was just the look of things.

Joe looked down at Jake sprawled out on the floor. He looked at the hand that did all the work, the hand that filled out the answers, and decided justice would be handled where justice was dealt. Joe lifted his foot and stomped on Jake's fingers. Jake screamed, but only Joe heard. He lifted his foot and brought it down again, and again and again. Jake could hear his bones crunching and cried in pain. Joe heard the same crunch which brought a smile to his face. This moment seemed to calm Joe down. He still hadn't said anything, but didn't feel he had to, Jake knew what this was about and hopefully he learned his lesson, if not, it would only get worse, and that was a Joe Luther guarantee.

Joe began to make his exit, while Jake lay sprawled in a pile of his own blood, that was growing larger as time passed. But before Joe left he thought it might be best to leave on a higher note. Just so they could both be certain on who was in charge of things. Joe turned back around, and delivered one final kick into Jakes face. Jake's head snapped back and smashed into the wall. From there it was lights out, see you later.

No one had to use the washroom for the rest of that lunch hour, and it wasn't until Jake failed to show up for class that any suspicion had arisen. And it wasn't until halfway through the afternoon when he was discovered by the janitor, when he was taking care of his cleaning duties. Doctors would have said he wouldn't have made it another ten minutes, and he was lucky to have been found when he was. But reality says he was much luckier, because when the janitor found him he was on his last minute, there was seconds left for him to be saved. But that's not luck at all, very far from it. Luck would have been not getting caught in such a situation in the first place.

Later that day Jake laid unconscious in the Fernwood hospital bed, with his mother and her tears by his side. The Doctor hadn't told her anything about his medical condition, mostly because he didn't know, but based on what he had seen in the past, he was afraid he was going to have to give her some terrible news, which he hated to do. So rather than tell her that, he thought it would be best not to tell her anything at all, at least until he had some more facts. Facts were what mattered, facts kept him safe, facts let him sleep at night. So he just let her keep on worrying. He was all right with that. As for Jake, he was about to enter a new world. A world no boy his age should ever have to be a part of, but the world he just left wasn't necessarily meant for a boy his age either. Not with the hell it just put him through. The funny part was, he hadn't gone through hell. Not yet.

4

Jake woke up in what appeared to be his home, in what appeared to be his bed, but things were different. They were backwards, and the colours weren't quite right. Some things were a little bit darker, while other things were a little bit brighter. The room was filled with an eerie silence, there wasn't noise coming from anywhere. For a moment he thought maybe he had lost his hearing but threw that theory out the window when he began to speak.

"Hello?" Jake called out. The sound of his voice startled him. He thought he sounded different, but he wasn't sure, he couldn't remember what he sounded like. He threw his legs over the bed, stood up and approached the bedroom door. He was curious to see what lay beyond there, he knew it wasn't going to be his house, and if it was, it was only going to be a resemblance of his house. The way the room he was in now was only a resemblance of his room. However, whatever laid beyond this door would remain a mystery at the moment, for when he reached it and held his hand out to turn the knob it wouldn't budge, Jake tried with all his might and nothing happened.

He tried turning it the other way with just as much success. He decided he would try the window, but when he tried to let go of the door knob it wouldn't let him, it was somehow holding on, almost as if there were thousands of tiny microscopic hands holding onto his. Jake began to panic, and as he panicked his grip got tighter, not on his own free will, it was his muscles acting all on their own. As his grip tightened the door knob began to heat up. It didn't take long for it to reach an uncomfortable temperature. He could see the door knob turning red as smoke began to rise between his fingers. Along with the smell of burning flesh, his burning flesh. He could feel the pain, but it didn't seem like the amount of pain he should have been feeling considering the situation, but he had never had this happen before so there wasn't much to compare it to.

Sweat began to drip down his face in a frenzy, but it wasn't just his face, he was sweating all over. It wasn't the panic that was causing the sweat, it was the room. The heat in the room was on the rise. It was as if there was a fire in the room, an invisible fire that didn't consume. He wanted to get to the window so bad, even more than that a glass of water. Jake closed his eyes and thought of a prayer. He was never brought to church, didn't know much about God, and he didn't know any prayers. So he did what he did best and made one up.

There was a loud bang, it sounded like thunder, but that's not what it was. The noise startled Jake, he opened his eyes before he could finish the prayer, to find his hands tightly clasped together. It wasn't the door he was holding onto anymore, it was just his other hand. He was holding them together so tight that they were giving off a small amount of heat. Not as much as a red hot door knob would give off, but there was some. Jake relaxed his hands and let them go. The room was still a fire and he was still incredibly thirsty. He went over to the window where he had planned to go when the door knob held him prisoner.

He flung open the curtains and looked out. There was nothing but darkness. It was as if the room he was in was just floating in the abyss. Panic had a hold of him once again and during this panic he came to a realization that the temperature of the room was beginning to drop. It began to plummet, he began to freeze. He looked at his hands. Only moments ago he was burning up and now his finger tips were turning numb. He went back to the bed and curled into a ball underneath the blankets. It was terrible. He could feel himself freezing into the position he was in, he wanted to stretch out but it was too cold. He began to feel something odd about the blanket, it was moving, it was slithering, it was alive. It wasn't the cold holding Jake into position, it was the blanket. Jake began to struggle as the blanket began to wrap tighter and tighter around him. The softness of it started to turn rough, similar to sandpaper, and it was getting tighter and rougher. Jake felt the pressure building up, his blood wasn't pumping properly anymore, he was beginning to feel light headed. And then, just before he was certain he was going to explode, the blanket tore. It just ripped and then disintegrated. With that, the room temperature went back to normal.

He stretched out and laid on the bed for a moment, wanting to get off before it turned into something else, but stayed on in fear of what could happen with any other part of the room he chose to venture. He was basically trying to figure out what it was that was going on. But before any actual thoughts were able to process, the room began shake.

It wasn't like an earthquake though, Jake had been in a few earthquakes, and this wasn't one. He didn't know what it was. It was as if the room was moving down a tunnel at an incredible speed. Nothing was moving in the room, no toys were falling, the pictures stayed perfectly still on the walls. Even the dreamcatcher hadn't.... it wasn't there, and then all at once Jake knew what was happening.

From outside the room he could hear a heard of animals, he wasn't sure what they were, they weren't making any sounds other than the thousands of footsteps rushing toward him. It got louder and louder as it approached the door. Jake hid his face in his hands awaiting the door to blow open and have whatever horror show it was make its grand entrance.

The sound was extremely loud now, Jake curled back up into a ball, covered his ears and screamed for it to stop. Then it did. Not because it went away, but because it was there. Waiting for him, on the other side of the door. But just like Jake, whatever was on the other side didn't know how to open it. He relaxed a bit, but not too much. He knew better.

Jake let go of his ears and let himself uncurl from his position. This time without a problem. He wanted to know what was on the other side. He reached his head as far as it could go without leaving the so-called comfort of the bed, to see if there was perhaps a shadow casting between the floor and the bottom of the door. Jake froze.

He was wrong, they didn't stop because they didn't know how to get in. They just slowed down so they could crawl under. Thousands and thousands of spiders were now entering the room and spreading out, filling as much space as they could as the moved forward. They had big brown nasty bodies and thick slimy pink legs covered with red thorns, and they were fast. They had already reached the bedside, but they weren't crawling up, maybe they didn't know how, that didn't matter though, because they were rising none the less. The room was filling up with them, soon he would be buried in a pile of these nasty creatures. Jake began to feel sick, he was going to vomit. He could feel it in the bottom of his stomach, he could feel it crawling up his throat, he could feel it crawling. Moments before he opened his mouth to let out whatever he last ate, he realized he could feel it crawling, and then it came. Thousands of spiders, exactly like the thousands that were filling the room shot out of his mouth and across the bed, covered with Jake's bodily fluids. The moment they landed they were turning around and heading back towards him.

Jake closed his eyes and did the only thing he could think of. He screamed, he cried and waited. He waited for something to happen, he waited for nothing to happen. He slowly opened his eyes again, to see what was next. The room was empty, the spiders were gone and the door was ajar. He could hear the sound of a piano being poorly played coming from outside the room. He peeked over the bed to be sure there were no critters. There were none. He looked back to the door and stood atop the bed. He had a fear something might grab him from underneath, but knew he had to get going. Jake crouched down and got ready to leap. He figured he could jump far enough across the room and make it out the door before whatever it was that was under the bed even knew he was gone. He took a deep breath, counted to three and leaped. For the first time things had seemed to work in his favour, because he jumped farther than he thought he ever had, or thought he could. He landed a few steps away from the door. Jake figured he was far enough that he had the time to look back. This was a bad idea, coming from under the bed was a hand, with an incredibly long skinny arm.

It was covered in rotting flesh, and it was directly behind him. Jake felt the boney fingers skim across his nose as it missed a grip on his face, Jake knew it wouldn't miss on its second attempt, he didn't even take the time to scream this time, just turned back to the door and ran. The fastest he ever ran in his entire life. That's when the laughter began, it was loud, it was coming from everywhere and it was laughing at him. He bolted out of the room and into the hall full speed. He was right about it being a different house. It wasn't a house at all. It was a cave with candles on the walls every ten feet. He still went forward though, He didn't want to know what was behind him, and he could feel it at his heels.

The music was still playing, it was terrible. As for the laughter, it began to fade away as Jake ventured farther and farther into the cave. There wasn't anywhere else to go but forward, it was just one long path that lead to wherever it was he was meant to be led.

As he got closer to the music the being that was chasing him no longer existed. This was good because Jake was getting tired and wanted to slow down, which he did and began to walk. It was much more peaceful now, Jake even felt a touch of love. He thought about looking behind him, just to be sure there wasn't anything there and when he did, there was nothing but a wall. He took a few steps forward and looked back again and the wall had crept up the same amount of steps he took. This time he stepped forward still watching the wall. The wall stayed where it was and then Jake was stopped. He had bumped into something, someone. He took a gulp, hoping it wasn't what was under the bed. He turned around to be somewhat relieved. It wasn't a monster, it was just a man.

He was tall, maybe 6'4, but to Jake everyone was tall, so this didn't have a crucial role in his perception. The man broke a smile. He had what appeared to be a mouthful of golden teeth. He was well dressed and appeared to be what one would call a distinguished gentleman.

"Hello Jake" the man said with an Australian accent, "I've been waiting for you." Jake didn't say anything, he didn't know what to say, he didn't feel anything, he didn't know what to feel.

"What's the matter? Cat got your tongue? Or maybe it was the spiders?" the man asked with a grin. Jake thought fear was his best option at this point.

"Oh my, I'm sorry, I didn't mean to frighten you, not right now anyway, allow me to introduce myself, my name is Oliver, and nothing else, just Oliver."

"I'm Jake" Jake managed to say with a tiny stutter.

"I know who you are Jake, I'm very well aware of you," Oliver paused, "you have something that belongs to me."

"I don't know what you're talking about," Jake said.

"No, I didn't think you would, Jake my friend, I've been around for a long long time, and I'll be around for a lot longer. I've spent my time doing things that aren't necessarily considered to be nice things, and I do them to nice people. I find this to be acceptable, do you know why?" Oliver asked, but Jake made no response. "It's because it's my nature, it's simply what I do. As God created man in his image, I was created in the image of darkness. Through the years I have been able to manipulate people to do some terrible things, mostly through their imaginations. The best way to get them is when they dream. A man can go to bed and wake up a completely different person, did you know that?

I've recruited certain souls over the years. The meanest of ones. Mostly because they ain't got no business going through those pearly gates in the sky. They come with me, they become my children." Oliver paused to think, then he carried on, "One of them is missing. Last I heard he was haunting the dreams of a young fellow by the name of Jake. Now this Jake found a way to keep him from tormenting him. I suppose to Jake, this is acceptable, but to me, it's quite the opposite."

"What are trying to say?" asked Jake

"Oh I'm not trying to say anything, what I'm saying is what I'm saying. You and me, we're going to make a deal. Right here, right now, and it comes highly recommended that you accept my offer." Oliver waited for Jake to make a response, but he chose not to speak, Oliver continued. "The dreamcatcher, a very effective piece of equipment, I must say. A nuisance, but effective. Do you understand what I'm getting at?"

"You want me to get rid of it?"

"Not quite, I want you to destroy it."

"but I like it."

"Yes, I can see why. It's a very beautiful piece, I was admiring it earlier."

"That's not why I like it, I like it because it won't let you bother me."

"That's not entirely true Jake. I'm fully capable of entering your reality. I was just under the impression that you were a reasonable boy."

"Then what's the problem?"

"The problem is my children are young and full of ignorance. They haven't been around long enough to understand the dangers of travelling from world to world. I only do it when it becomes completely necessary. Other than that, the dream is the best way to go, there's not much danger in a dream, I assume you're familiar with a spider web." Oliver watched Jake nod his head and carried on, "The intention of the web is to catch the fly, and the fly stays caught. That's until the spider comes along and completes the circle of life, but until that moment, the fly stays caught.

The dreamcatcher works in a similar way. The only difference is, there is no spider to come along and complete the circle. Even if there was, there'd be no circle to complete. After life its death forever.

My child is caught in the webs of your catcher. Now he's strong, he was a big boy. He's struggling to get out, but it's hard. He won't give up though, so he's got that going for him. I want you to remember that.

Whatever is going on between the two of you is strictly business of your own, but as of right now, I'm giving you the opportunity to completely neutralize the entire situation."

"How are you going to do that?" Jake asked.

"It's simple. Right now, in your world, you are in the Fernwood hospital. You've been there for a week and you haven't woke up. They don't have much hope for you, but as long as they keep the machines on, you'll stay alive. What they don't know is I'm in charge of if and when you wake up,

I got complete control over that. So this is what I want you to do. You wake up, go home and release my child from his prison. Thus completing the relationship between all three of us." "And if I say no?" Jake asked

"Then you stay in here, with me, that's until they decide to let you die. After that you'll probably head on up to the big kingdom. I control time here though, and I could make it last forever, just you me and them." Oliver pointed behind Jake, Jake turned around and saw the wall which was now full of the spiders. Jake turned back to Oliver.

"Okay, how do I do it?" Jake asked.

"It's simple, just cut the strings," Oliver said.

"Okay," Jake agreed, "but I just want to know one thing."

"I'm sure you do."

"Why was it me? Why am I the one being terrorized?"

"Aww Jake, it's nothing personal. It's just you happen to live on the land that wasn't meant for living. You want to blame somebody, blame the people that moved back there. In recent history there was a major event that proved evil's existence. After that, anyone who lives there deserves what they got coming."

Jake took a moment to try and understand what he had just heard. He didn't have the slightest clue what Oliver was talking about. He would be sure to investigate the history of the town when he got out of this place. He wouldn't find out much though. The town tended to keep their secrets as a whole quite well. When Jake was done thinking, he brought his attention back to Oliver.

"Can you wake me up now?" Jake asked.

"Not yet, not before I give you my warning. I know people Jake, and I know not to trust people. You don't want to screw me over, I understand you can sleep under that dreamcatcher and not be touched by me or any one of us. But I know my ways around, and I have ways of seeing you to sleep without that thing in your presence. Just as I have proven most recently. If I catch you at that time should you chose to be so silly and make the mistake of not following through with your end of the bargain, your hell will begin forever. You follow?"

"I wouldn't even think about it" Jake said. Oliver smiled, he had a sense about people when they were lying, and was quite certain Jake was telling the truth. He didn't look like the type to tell a lie. However Oliver was wrong from time to time.

5

Jake laid in his hospital bed with his mother by his side that Thursday morning. It had been two weeks since the school incident. Time has a interesting way of moving when your lost in other worlds. Nobody had a clue who did it to him. Well they had a clue, but they had no proof and unless Jake woke up and pointed a finger, there was nothing to be done about it. His mother wasn't concerned about him pointing a finger though, she was more concerned about him waking up. Which was what he did.

She was sitting beside his bed dozing off, with his hand in hers, she had sat there for quite some time. She felt a huge load of guilt pass through her whenever she ever left, she wanted to be there when he woke up. She knew he would wake up, because she had faith, and that's what faith does.

She didn't notice Jake open his eyes, but she did feel his fingers close around her hand. At first she thought it was just her imagination, a dream seeping into reality from the lack of sleep she had been getting, but when she looked up and saw his eyes looking back at her she knew. Jake was back.

She shouted with joy, it echoed all through the hospital corridor, it wasn't long before a nurse had come in and seen the miracle. To them that's what it was. She immediately rushed out of the room to find a doctor, who came in about five minutes after Jake had first opened his eyes in a return to the real world, or what they thought was the real world. He was bombarded with many questions from the nurse, the doctor and his mother, but he wasn't up to answering any of them. The only words that came out of his mouth that day were, "I need the dreamcatcher." His mother still didn't want to leave his side, but the look of desperation in Jake's eyes allowed her to make an exception.

Jake spent another week in the hospital during his recovery, with his dreamcatcher hung above the bed. He was doing quite well. He ate his proper meals, got his proper exercise, and his proper rest. He slept well, undisturbed.

If what he went through wasn't all in his imagination he assumed Oliver was a little pissed off right now, but Jake knew that wasn't necessary. Jake knew what needed to get done and he knew exactly how to do it.

A couple of days had passed while Jake remained in the hospital. His mother still spent a majority of her time there, but the bills needed to be paid, and with her being the only one responsible for such situations, she went back to work.

One of the afternoons while his mother was gone Mr. Anderson, who was the school principal, and Mrs. Marsman who was the school counselor, walked in. Jake was sitting up in his bed watching a national geographic program on the television.

"Hey Jake," said Mr. Anderson, "how are you doing?" Jake turned his attention to his new guests.

"I'm doing fine," Jake said.

"That's good to hear son," Mr. Anderson seemed pleased, "you know we all miss you at the school." Jake didn't know how to respond to this so he said nothing. This made Mr. Anderson feel a bit awkward. "Listen, we wanted to ask you a few questions about what happened in the boy's washroom, how do you feel about that?"

"The doctors and nurses already asked me about that, and so did my mom, I'm not sure what else you want to know." Jake said. Mr. Anderson took a step back and looked at Mrs. Marsman letting her know it was her turn to talk, there was no hesitation.

"Jake, we know you can't remember everything, but if it was Joe who did this to you we need to know, he's a bit of a troubled child and if you don't speak up, he won't learn a valuable lesson and he'll carry on with his ways. Which is only going to escalate and most likely lead to murder one day?"

"Mrs. Marsman," Jake said, "I'm not sure I understand what your trying to say, I find it very confusing as to why you all think Joe is responsible for whatever it was that happened in there, and I find it odd you would accuse him of committing a murder that hasn't even taken place yet. Joe's not a bad guy, he's my friend and even more so, he's my only friend. Now I don't think my mother would be too impressed if she found out you two came down here, asking the questions you chose to ask. So I think it might be best for you to leave, and I mean that in the most respectful way, but in all honesty I find it truly offensive what you have just spoken to me" Jake paused to look at the stunned expression that was left on both of their faces. When nobody moved or said a thing he continued, "in other words, I'll see you when I return to class." Jake turned his attention back to the television as Mr. Anderson and Mrs. Marsman stared at each other in sheer confusion. When they realized they had made a mistake coming there, they both walked out the door without a word to anyone.

A week later Jake was back home, he was healing at an exceptional rate. His mother felt he would be fit to return to school after the weekend, which was what he did. This was the moment he was waiting for. On the day he woke up with plans to return to class he did everything he would have done on any regular day that he went to school.

He went to the kitchen, and had himself a bowl of cereal. He thought he might be getting bacon and pancakes, but he thought wrong. His mother was just too busy. She was behind with work after spending so much time with him at the hospital, and she needed to work a bunch of overtime to make up for it. She wasn't mad about it, these were the things that happen in life and she understood that. That's what makes life what it is, nothing is ever clockwork.

Once Jake had finished his breakfast, he went back to his room to pack his bag for school. He had all of his books stacked neatly on his desk. He had enough time over the weekend to get everything organized. It didn't take him very long because most of his belongings were kept in an organized fashion. After he had gathered all of his belongings he walked over to his bed.

He was now gazing at his dreamcatcher. It was back above his bed. The first thing his mother had done when he got home from the hospital was hang it back up there. Jake made sure of that. He loved it, it was beautiful, it was hypnotizing, but a deal is a deal and that's all there was to it. Jake unhooked it from the wall above his bed where it would never hang again, and put it into his back pack. Then it was off to school.

When he arrived at the bus stop he knew everything had returned back to normal. At least what normal was to him, the future whorish girls sang there dumb songs and made fun of a certain persons situation. No morals or ethics these girls had, but maybe it was all right for them to do what they needed to do for fun right now, because their futures weren't bright at all.

Everything went well for Jake on his first morning back, the students were extra kind to him, and the teachers showed their concerns. During the morning gym class, Mrs. Marsman asked Jake to join her in her office. Jake didn't really want to, but not being a fan of physical education he thought, "What the heck." and went to see what she had to say.

As he would have guessed, it was just the same old question about who did what to him in the washroom, and he stuck to his same old story of not remembering a thing. He even took the time to add in the fact that he was excited to see Joe. He couldn't wait, and this time he was telling the truth. This comment troubled her, but at the same time she paid it no mind.

Then it was time for lunch, the moment Jake was waiting for. Jake sat alone at the table he usually sat alone at. Some children asked if he would mind if they sat with him, but he declined, he would rather eat alone. That was until Joe came along, He didn't ask to sit down, he just came and sat.

"Hey Jake," Joe said, not in his usual bully voice, this was the voice of a friend, but Jake didn't notice that.

"Joe" Jake acknowledged him and took another bite of his sandwich, he was waiting for Joe to take something or criticize his meal, but this never happened. It seemed Joe finally felt bad about something.

"Listen, I wanted to apologize about... well about you know" Joe said. Jake listened but made no response. "You have a right to be upset"

"Upset?" Jake asked, "Upset about what?"

Joe looked puzzled, perhaps he did beat him bad enough that Jake really didn't remember any of what happened.

"I just want you to know things are going to be different now, between you and me" Joe said with sincerity

"Oh I know," Jake replied as he took the last bite of his sandwich, and got up from the table to make his exit. He was almost going to just walk away, he knew Joe was different now, but it didn't change the fact that he did what he did, and chances were he'd end up doing it again. Rage has a way of taking over oneself at moments of weakness, and Joe was the type to be weak. On top of that, he had a deal to keep.

"Oh I almost forgot," Jake said as he reached into his pocket. Joe just sat and watched, "this is for you." Jake pulled his hand out of his pocket in a fist and held it out, "kind of a token, for our friendship." Jake said as Joe reached out his hand and held his palm out, curious and suspicious at the same time. Jake opened his hand and let out a pile of blue threads. They fell into Joe's hands and that was all it took. Joe didn't know though, at least not at the time, whether or not he knows now is hard to tell. Jake smiled and left the cafeteria, never looking back. While Joe just stared at him the whole time, the same way he stared the last time he saw him exit the cafeteria. Only this time there was no rage, it had been replaced with sorrow and confusion.

The next day Joe never made it to class, nor the day after, or the day after that. Teachers never said anything about what had happened. Rumors began to circulate. It started from the kids who lived in Joe's neighborhood. They would talk about a nurse showing up at his house on a daily basis, all the way up until the time they took him away. Not because the house was unfit for him, (which it was) but because he had become too unfit for society.

When they walked him out of his house, they said he had the face of someone who hadn't slept for months, it was the face of a man who aged thirty years while still being contained in an eight year olds body. Every single hair on his head was as white as snow. He spoke, but it didn't make much sense, strange ramblings, and tiny screams. They could make out one word though, but nobody knew what it meant. "Oliver." But those were only the rumors.

As for Jake, Jake did just fine. His marks remained above average all through his school years. He never became accustomed to physical education. He had his good days along with the bad ones, but never getting as bad as it had before. As for the dreamcatcher, it was gone, he didn't know where, and didn't care. Over time he forgot about it completely. He never got a new one, he never had to, because every night, for the next seventy eight years of his life, Jake slept like a baby.

Braxton's Notes

Before you close these pages and carry on with the lives you live in your world. I'd like to say a few names of the people I would like to thank. These are the people who played a crucial role for me to get this book complete, whether they knew it or not.

Al Harris
Andrew Morrison
Trevor Olson
Sharon Harris
Chelsey Scully
Morgan Fenske
Cordell Johnson
Jon Friesen
Cody Ford
Shawn Mcmurray
Matthew Mackarell
Courtney Marsman
Andre Douglas

Feng Feng San
Barb Brown
Daniel Jones
Amanda Spowart
Johnathon Radcliffe
Brandon Nepper
Shea
And of course you, yourself, the reader.

Thank you for your time and consideration.

Printed in the United States
By Bookmasters